WINNER
OF THE DRUE HEINZ
LITERATURE PRIZE

1983

# PRIVATE PARTIES

JONATHAN PENNER

UNIVERSITY OF PITTSBURGH PRESS

Published by the University of Pittsburgh Press, Pittsburgh, Pa. 15260
Copyright © 1983 by Jonathan Penner
All rights reserved
Feffer and Simons, Inc., London
Manufactured in the United States of America

Library of Congress Cataloging in Publication Data

Penner, Jonathan, 1940-
    Private parties.

    I. Title.
    PS3566.E477P7 1983         813'.54         83-47825
    ISBN 0-8229-3488-4

"Amarillo" first appeared in *TriQuarterly*. "Articles on the Heart" was originally published in *Kansas Quarterly*. "At Center" is reprinted from *The Louisville Review*. "Emotion Recollected in Tranquillity" originally appeared in *Quarterly West*. "Frankenstein Meets the Ant People" is reprinted from *Antaeus*. "Harry and Maury" first appeared in *The Literary Review*. "Investments" and "Sailing Home" originally appeared in *Harper's Magazine*. "Men Are of Three Kinds" first appeared in *The North American Review*. "Shrinkage" originally appeared in *Denver Quarterly*. "Temblor" was first published in *California Quarterly*. "Things To Be Thrown Away" first appeared in *The Yale Review*. "Uncle Hersh" is reprinted from *Prairie Schooner*. "A Way of Life" originally appeared in *Story Quarterly*.

*I thank the John Simon Guggenheim Memorial Foundation,*
*the National Endowment for the Arts,*
*and the Arizona Commission on the Arts*
*for their generous support.*

TO MY FATHER

# CONTENTS

*Private Parties*

# Men Are of Three Kinds

MY GRANDFATHER IS VALIANT AS the lion, churlish as the bear. No man hath a virtue that he hath not a glimpse of. Nor any man an attaint but he carries some stain of it. Shakespeare, *Troilus and Cressida*. He is seventy-six years old and many times a millionaire. He wears in Scarsdale what he wears in Florida, creamwhite shoes, trousers the shining lime of a sourball on the tongue. He is a man of action.

On the patio in Scarsdale he sits, always with people, always talking. By profession he is—still, at his age—a finder. What does he find? Companies! He makes a pharmaceutical midget enter the mouth of a chemical giant. He extracts from the emperor of ice cream the bride-price of a brewery. For this he earns commissions in the hundreds of thousands of dollars. We couldn't live his life for an hour.

In lime trousers and champagne shirt he sits on his patio, talking. We are visiting from Ohio, my father and I, after my college graduation. *What is this man?* Is there any Chairman of the Board he doesn't know, any necessary politician who never sat where I'm sitting now?

"I'm on the road next week," he says. "United Brands is going to buy Dubuque Beef. They don't know it yet." He will represent the Beef, a man his age who built the business, who was here a month ago sitting in my cast-iron chair. "United, those dopes. I offered them Bic Pens for four million. Procter and Gamble just bought it for eight times that."

Money! He lives for it, the deals he made and—even more—the ones he missed. "Martin," he tells my father, "you remember. Remember? I went to Inland Steel, I had American Chain and Cable in my pocket. Five years they'd have tripled their investment. Dopes!"

His man Horacio drives us into the city the next morning. Grandfather needs to see his bankers, who are growing too conservative. My father, a historian, is attending a scholarly conference. I am going to the New York Public Library, to pace off the walls of alphabetized index cards, to smell the books somebody wrote now abandoned in millions, to see innumerable people who'd still be here if I closed my eyes.

When I return by train and cab, anesthetic with sensation, they are still awake, though my father just barely. His jowls swell against his neck, his eyes look stapled half-open. My grandfather's day has not been good. "A *kid* comes in," he says, "your age, Bobby, and tells me my client's credit's no good. I tell him, listen: you get out of that chair and go straight to Jack Bergen, who I've dealt with longer than you've been alive. You tell Jack if he's responsible for this attack of gutlessness, which I can't believe, he isn't killing me, he's killing himself."

We are sitting on the flagstone patio. No moon, no stars—why is it so light? At the far end of a woodchip path, lined by topiary camels whose lightbulb hearts shine faint blue, lies the great pool in its scalloped shell. It's heated. I can see the rising steam.

"I thought Jack Bergen had died," says my father, massaging his eyelids. "Last year. A stroke."

"Take a dip," my grandfather urges me. He and my father have already been. They are robed and toweled, drinking Scotch.

"Pull off your clothes right here," he says. "Show us what being young is like." I stand away in the dark. To the southwest, the sky is bottom-lit as though New York will clear the trees. "Good," my grandfather says, "very good," and naked I trot the woodchip path. Ahead of me the pool shimmers as cleaning tendrils dance blindly in its depth. In midleap I will live forever: this is promised to be mine.

"The human brain," my father says, "comprises roughly twelve billion neurons. That's in a young adult such as yourself."

It's winter break, and we are visiting my grandfather on Palm Key. But Horacio was putting his suitcase into the car when we arrived. "Japan," said my grandfather, putting down his elephant-hide attaché case, immediately picking it up again. "Mitsubishi is going to buy Firestone. I forgot you were coming. Why don't you have Horacio take you out for some fishing?"

"Each day," says my father, "a hundred thousand neurons die." We are sitting in the skylit Florida kitchen because, without my grandfather here, the other downstairs rooms are too big; they make us feel like burglars. "The brain shrinks." My father makes patting, squeezing gestures in midair, like a boy compacting a snowball. The telephone in the kitchen rings and is answered in some far part of the house.

He lowers his folded hands to the kitchen table. Across from him, I imitate his posture, an urge that I sometimes find irresistible. Emulation? Parody? I don't know! In a moment he will reach for his three-ring notebook and ballpoint pen, Ohio objects that look very strange here, and suggest we jot a few things down.

A man of reason. Each day he carries a list, prepared the night before, of things he must do. His calendar has blue-inked notes such as, on my birthday, "Robert b." Blue notes on the dates my mother was b, he and she were m, and she d. I can't believe I remember her, but there's a hand cream whose scent means that I do. Blue-inking his past into his future, while sipping one glass of still white wine, is his ceremony each New Year's Eve.

Horacio appears, impressive in his thick shoulders and dark mustache. He points at my father, who picks up the kitchen phone. Then he hands my father what look like airline tickets. I can tell who it is because the shouting makes my father hold the phone away from his ear. "I will," he says. "Drink some water. Loosen your tie. It's all right."

In a minute a quieter voice comes on. "Yes sir," says my father. He says that when I wish he wouldn't, to minority guys who think he's being ironic. "I apologize for the trouble, sir," he says, and reads a lot of numbers from the tickets. He scratches an ankle. All my father's socks are the same gray-black, so a hole in one won't ruin a pair. "No," he says, "only excited."

When he hangs up he looks at me a long time, stroking his beard. Then he says, "Let's jot a few things down," and reaches for his notebook and pen.

"Senior, senator, and senile are all from the Latin, signifying old." He carefully makes a checkmark on the blank page.

There's a lot of money involved here," I say. "Do you feel he's steady?"

"Characterized by loss of memory." Check. Check. "Loss of mathematical ability."

"Do you feel," I ask, "that he could do something radical?"

"Disorientation in time and place."

Now there are four little hooks on his page. He frowns at them. I frown at them. I feel a strange rightness, an inevitability, in this scene: we have always enjoyed having a table between us. When the telephone rings I look up, but he's lost in thought, stroking his beard. The ringing stops. I tell him, "I've got a suggestion, I guess."

Though the trust fund is entirely mine—my father gets the interest during his lifetime—I was surprised that he wouldn't help me. He didn't oppose me, either. Before we left Florida, my grandfather's legal residence, I talked to a lawyer who earns his Porsches from non compos mentis. The bank is my grandfather's conservator. The New York and Florida houses are sold.

Now he lives across the street in our Ohio college town. Beyond the Pump-Ur-Self station, cornfields begin, which to him is fascinating and bizarre. Horacio came too but left in the first winter, when it stayed below freezing for weeks. My grandfather's content now, but lonely. He has dinner with us every night.

I come in from running or ice-skating—I need to do something every day—from the freezing outside into the warm house, and I feel so alive it's unbearable. Twenty-two years old! Twelve billion neurons! I think of being my grandfather's age, or even my father's. I pretend my legs and back are stiff, and I can't hear well, and I stick out my stomach as though I'm getting fat. For a second or two it seems real—like when I pretend I'm blind by closing my eyes—but later I haven't learned anything.

In the evening, after dinner, we sit in the living room, draperies open so we can look out at the falling, rising snow. The windward sides of trees and telephone poles are plastered with it. To leeward it lies in arcs that look drawn with a draftsman's curve. It swarms like moths around the streetlamps. When a car passes, catching a pedestrian in its headlights, the blown snow whirls so thickly around him that he looks legless, his angled upper half gliding along on foam.

"Amana Home Freezers," says my grandfather. "I came to General Electric with Amana in my pocket. Those stupid dopes! I showed them Maytag washers, too. I had Fred Maytag in the palm of my hand."

"A solid machine," says my father. He is only half paying attention, glancing up now and then from a stack of exam booklets, tapping them with his red ballpoint pen. He tells me, "Your mother always liked the Maytag. They cost a bundle but they were extremely well made."

"Still are," my grandfather insists sleepily, and sips his Scotch, content. I can feel his contentment. I suddenly know that when he was twenty-two he never locked his knees and elbows, stiffened his muscles until they cramped, to see what being old might be like. My father, perhaps, once squinted till the world blurred, and once was enough. Only a man of feeling needs to bind his days together. Our bathroom has a mirror over the sink and one mounted on the opposite wall. I stand between them before I take my shower, a regiment of Roberts, doing in space what I want to do in time.

When spring comes, and my father has a symposium in New York, and I want to go too, we check my grandfather into a residential care facility, just for the week. He's still clear enough—he knows who we are—but now gets lost a block from home. I ask him whether he wants me to visit his old house in Scarsdale, and he says no, no point to that.

The day after we get to New York, I rent a car and drive out. The house is freshly painted, an unfamiliar pastel, and the new owner has lined the long driveway with beds of flowers. At least a dozen dogwoods have been planted. A gardener is riding a groaning lawn tractor back and forth among them, spreading something white from a hopper. Seeing me watching from my car, he waves. I wonder what the new people have done behind the house, whether the swimming pool still shimmers and steams at the end of its woodchip path. I can more easily imagine it vanished than still there.

The gardener waves again and I look at him closely. To my utter amazement, it's Horacio! I recognize his shock of hair and black mustache, his perpetually beard-stippled cheeks, his broad bowed shoulders. I feel as happy and relieved as though I've found the afterlife. Though he and I have never been particularly close, I run up to embrace him. He sees me coming with outstretched arms and dismounts from his tractor but doesn't shut off its engine. The roaring moment before I reach him, I realize that it isn't Horacio at all, in fact looks nothing like him—this is no gardener, I can tell, this is the new owner himself, starting to open his mouth, an enormous, thickly wrinkled man—but now he's opened his arms too, clearly mistaking who I am, persuaded by my joyous rush, and now it's too late for either of us to stop.

# Uncle Hersh

THAT SPRING, THE THEN CONGRESS-
man Dvorsky invited my parents and me to his
son's circumcision. I was home from college for
vacation and had never seen one. Now I'm in Senator
Dvorsky's family, and can get favors from federal agencies,
but forget the favors.

Dvorsky's place on Long Island Sound was what people
who aren't wealthy call a mansion. Jammed, which I hated
at that age, and full of smoke. There was a slim girl with
oversized horn-rimmed glasses and her hair back tight in a
barrette, Dvorsky's niece, looking out the window at a big
Labrador on the beach.

"He's mine," she told me. Her voice was quiet and
cautious, as though she thought I might disagree. I felt like
telling jokes or bringing her a glass of cold orange juice.
Somebody called and all the men went into another room,
where we pressed together, and something happened in the
middle that I couldn't see, and a baby screamed. We
drifted back. I had my drink freshened at the bar.

"Did you see that butcher?" a short, hunched man with

wild hair kept asking. He seemed enraged. He wandered around the living room, his bulging eyes flashing from face to face. "I never saw such blood. Listen to that kid."

"Shush," said a woman.

He shouted, "Shush? After what I saw?"

The woman turned away. He came to the window, grabbed me by the biceps. "I didn't see it," I apologized. He stared up at me, his forehead working. Burst blood vessels had stained the whites of his eyes.

"Uncle Hersh, did he do it wrong?" asked the cautious girl. He made a skewering gesture. "Should we do something?" she asked.

He shrugged. "Try and tell them. The kid's bleeding like a stuck pig."

Janet and her sisters had been orphans, and their Uncle Bert had been able to take two, with Janet left over for Uncle Hersh. She lived with him and Aunt Florence in a smaller house next door that had once been the servants' quarters for Uncle Bert's place. Now Uncle Bert was Congressman Dvorsky and Uncle Hersh was a middle-level executive at Pepperidge Farm, some big deal. "Just because he's sick a lot they won't promote him," Janet said. "They don't appreciate Uncle Hersh. He cares about the tiniest detail."

He was back, the ice cubes jingling aggressively in his glass, his forehead laced with sweat. "No one can say we weren't here," he told Janet. "Let's walk."

"Beautiful," said Janet.

"I walk every day, sometimes twice," Uncle Hersh told me. "Otherwise my guts don't work." I introduced myself. "Come as far as the lobster house," he urged. "Let's see what they're doing on a Sunday afternoon."

We walked along the shore road, Janet's Labrador prancing around us and trying to poke his nose into our crotches. I said I went to school in New Jersey. Uncle Hersh said he had been born there, and still went back to visit his parents' graves. "How do you drive?" he asked. "Take the G. W. Bridge?"

"Tappan Zee," I said.

He nodded. "Then shoot across the Cross Westchester Expressway."

"To the Turnpike."

"Beats the Parkway."

When we reached the lobster house he counted the cars in the parking lot. "It's not the season, and look at that," he said. "I bet they've opened the upstairs."

"Uncle Hersh had a chance to buy in," Janet explained.

"Sixteen years ago. But lobsters? You eat lobsters?"

"Never," I admitted.

He looked up at me fiercely, tossing the hair back from his big gleaming eyes. Then he shuddered. "Just the thought of eating a lobster makes me sick," he said.

That summer was the summer of the beach. Janet browned to the shade of pancakes and I thought about rubbing butter on her. Aunt Florence believed we were

sleeping together. Sometimes, bicycling into their driveway on a still morning, I could hear Janet and her aunt
trying to shout in whispers. They didn't want to bother
Uncle Hersh, who was sick most of that summer.

"She's nothing but a shrew," said Janet. But when she
was calmer she tried to explain Aunt Florence to me.
"She's an adventurous and talented woman. And she married a man who just fusses."

The summer passed. The spot where Janet's glasses
dented the bridge of her nose remained untanned, and I
wanted to protect it with my fingertips. In the early
evenings we walked to the lobster house. The parking lot
was always full, and the line of summer residents waiting to
be seated reached to the front steps. Sometimes we walked
there along the beach, cooling our ankles in the low tide.
The wall of the lobster house facing the Sound was mostly
glass. We could see the people inside eating and drinking.
When it got dark the waiters lit candles. Behind us the
Sound was sighing. I was twenty. The sky? The stars?
Please.

When we got back, Uncle Hersh, lying on the living
room sofa, would ask if the lobster house seemed busy.
Then he grimaced and said he was through caring. About
anything. Savagely, with the edge of his hand, he chopped
at the sofa cushions. "Be meticulous, work like a dog.
Sacrifice yourself."

"Uncle Hersh types all his own correspondence," Janet
said.

"I won't sign a sloppy letter. No typos, not one. Secretaries can't meet those standards. You're imposing on them."

He had a rheumatic heart, he told me. "I risk my life for Pepperidge Farm every day. You think I'm a stockholder? From now on I let it slide, all of it."

"Like an elephant flies," said Aunt Florence.

Uncle Hersh tossed his head wildly and chopped at the sofa again. Dust flew up and he coughed. The Labrador, lying beside him, barked once and thumped its tail on the floor. Janet went for water. "You can't trust anybody," Uncle Hersh said. "Anything you want done right, do it yourself." He reached up to grab me by the biceps but his grip slipped. "I'll tell you something. Janet trusts everyone. You watch her."

"Janet's an adult," said Aunt Florence.

"She doesn't count her change."

"People usually give you too much, not too little," said Janet, coming back with the water.

He grabbed the glass fiercely but drank only a sip. "I won't leave a toll booth until I count every nickel."

July 4th, and Congressman Dvorsky rode through town in a motorcade. Later he borrowed Uncle Hersh's outdoor grill and posed for photographs in a chef's hat. That evening, Aunt Florence and Janet and I sat on the beach and watched the fireworks. Uncle Hersh narrowed his eyes scornfully and said, "Incredible," but later I saw him at a window. August came and he was back at work, furious at how things had been handled in his absence. August ended. "Driving back to Jersey?" he asked.

I hated it, but I was. We talked highways for a while because I knew how much he enjoyed that. Aunt Florence hugged me, relieved that I was going but feeling guilty over it and liking me, I could tell. Janet and I took a long drive. When we got back the house was dark. No sign of life but the sleepy Labrador, which rose from the lawn to lick our hands.

That fall we wrote letters. I was in New Jersey, she was in Ohio. You leave a place and you begin to question what happened there.

It was Thanksgiving before we were together again at Uncle Hersh's. There was no question after all. We became engaged. But it seemed easier not to tell anyone until we had more time—at Christmas, we decided.

Uncle Hersh looked well and almost happy. At dinner he hunched low, shoveling it in, his chin almost on his plate, his bulging eyes flashing up at me again and again.

He quizzed me. About every course, every teacher, where I lived, how much rent I paid, what I ate and didn't it clog my guts, what octane gas I used and what weight oil. I mentioned that this time I had taken the George Washington Bridge and the Cross Bronx Expressway and the Hutchinson River Parkway and the New England Turnpike. "The fastest, right?" he said. "I'd like to see you try that on a holiday weekend before they finished the Bruckner Interchange."

After dinner, Janet and Uncle Hersh and I took a walk. Aunt Florence said it was too cold and made him wear a scarf, but when we got outdoors he ripped it off and threw it at the Labrador. We walked past Uncle Bert's house, which was dark—to keep the reporters away, Uncle Hersh said. This was the year that questions were being asked about Congressman Dvorsky's tax returns.

Janet said she was sure he had cheated. "If I had his money," said Uncle Hersh, "I'd do the same thing. It's disgusting, though. Just thinking about it makes me sick."

"I might do that," I said. "But not you."

"I've done plenty," he said angrily. "Years back." He jabbed a thumb into his stomach. "I had a bellyful. I couldn't take it, that's what's wrong with me. Now, Bert. It's his kind that runs the world."

"You'd be a better Congressman," said Janet.

He stopped on the sidewalk and threw both arms into the air. "Typing my own letters? You know what it takes to be a Congressman? Sloppiness, letting things happen any way they want. Just letting it happen. That's the secret." A car bright with chrome raced by with a roar. "Slow down," he screamed after it.

He walked on and we followed him. Soon we came to the lobster house, where a sign suggested reservations for Thanksgiving dinner. "Sometimes," Uncle Hersh said, "I want to line them all up against that wall." He pointed to the lobster house. "And take a tommygun." His body jerked as he fired it.

We turned to walk back. Something bad happened then.

Janet's Labrador was killed. The car with all the chrome came racing back with mufflers roaring. Janet screamed as the Labrador danced into the road and was crushed.

"Look at that," said Uncle Hersh. Then the Labrador raised its head and made a sound. Uncle Hersh said, "You got a jackknife?" I didn't. He found a rock and went up to the dog. When he came back he was coughing.

The car had skidded and slowed and stopped. Now it was coming back toward us, roaring in reverse gear. The driver was no high school kid but a big greaseball in denim. Uncle Hersh was holding Janet. I had gone to look at the dog and came back as the guy walked up. "Jesus," he said. "I'm sorry."

"You're drunk," said Uncle Hersh. He had stopped coughing but was still breathing hard.

"No, man."

"Let's see your license."

"You ain't a cop. Listen, I'll pay for the dog, you name it."

"I don't want your money," said Uncle Hersh. He walked very close, head cocked back. His chin was practically in the guy's chest as he panted and stared up at him. "I want your license. I want you off the road."

The greaseball looked at his car and you could see that driving it meant everything to him. He walked back to it with Uncle Hersh after him. "You don't want money that's it," he said. "I offered, you refused, finito."

Uncle Hersh lay down in the road and stuck both legs

under the car. "Get the plate number and call the cops," he told me. "He runs over dogs but he won't break a man's legs."

The big guy grabbed Uncle Hersh under the arms but couldn't budge him. "I've got my feet hooked around your drive shaft," Uncle Hersh said. "In a minute you'll be holding a stiff. I have a heart condition."

I ran back to the lobster house and made the phone call. A newspaper photographer came with the police. Uncle Hersh, half under the car, folded his arms and glared at the camera. Congressman Dvorsky made a phone call that night, and the picture was never published.

That winter, back at college, Janet wrote that for two years she had had a love affair with one of her professors. She wouldn't have told me, but if we got married it would be something her friends knew and she was afraid I would hear about it. She thought I should know before Christmas, when we planned to announce our engagement. She had put off telling me as long as she could.

When I read that letter it made me feel a way I hated, as though she had poison ivy or something and wanted to borrow some lotion and I didn't want to give it to her. Then I did something stupid. I visited a prostitute. Don't ask me why. After that I wanted to see Janet very much, and wrote her that I was glad she'd told me and that I would like it if we didn't ever have to talk about it again.

When we met at home during Christmas vacation I

thought she looked beautiful, but sad. Uncle Hersh wasn't feeling well again, and Aunt Florence was worried about him. He was still working but often seemed short of breath. His eyes looked brighter and more bulging than ever. At dinner he ate less, and his gestures were subdued, and sometimes I saw sweat running down his forehead when I didn't feel hot at all. Janet and I decided to wait to announce our engagement. It would be better to tell them when everybody was relaxed.

New Year's Eve came, and Congressman Dvorsky was having a party too big for his home. He had rented the whole upstairs of the lobster house. Uncle Hersh bared his teeth at that and grabbed his chest with both hands, rocking back and forth. "We'll stay here," said Aunt Florence. "I have sherry and cheese."

But Uncle Hersh felt well all day, better and better through the evening. "I'm going over and see the circus," he insisted, with a sneer, close to midnight. So we all went. It was snowing, and this time he kept his scarf on. Nevertheless he was wheezing when we got there.

The upstairs of the lobster house was loud with music and full of smoke and jammed with the Congressman's friends. I didn't know anyone, and Janet knew very few. We four stayed together like delegates to a hostile power. At midnight, Aunt Florence gave me a warm kiss, and Janet gave me a soft kiss. I drank too much. Uncle Hersh drank much too much.

Another hour and the crowd had thinned. The snow was

heavy now, and some were worried about getting home. That was a polite excuse, said the Congressman, looking around. Most of them were going on to other parties.

But Uncle Hersh wasn't ready to go. He got me off to the side. "The Parkway will be closed," he said. "They'll be able to keep the Turnpike open."

"One lane, anyway," I agreed. "I'd hate to be on the Cross County tonight."

"Or the Hutch. God, there are a lot of roads. I was trying to count up. Coming from Jersey you could take the Henry Hudson past the Cloisters, cut over to the Deegan, New York State Throughway to Hartsdale, then the Expressway over to the Turnpike. Or cut through the Bronx, Grand Concourse to Mosholu Parkway and Gun Hill Road, then out the Post Road."

"Too many lights."

He shook himself all over, tossed his hair, panted up at me. "You wouldn't. But you could, that's what gets me. Right this minute there are people driving on every one of those roads."

I nodded quickly. "Where are they all going. I think about that all the time."

Uncle Hersh stamped his foot in rage and slopped his drink on both of us. "No," he shouted. "That's not my point!"

"Then what is your point," I shouted back, wounded.

He grabbed my jacket, pulled me very close. His big eyes were like searchlights on my face. "How do you know," he said, knocking his fist against my chest with every word. "How do you choose which road you want, what difference does it make. That's my point. You get me now?"

I nodded uncertainly. He let go in disgust and pushed me away.

Now Congressman Dvorsky walked up and said that everyone was leaving. He was driving back and had room for us in his car.

In the parking lot we crowded into the big sedan, the Congressman in front with his family, Uncle Hersh and Janet and Aunt Florence and I in back. The car's windows were covered with snow.

"Give me the scraper," said Uncle Hersh. "I'll go around."

His brother turned on the wipers and in a minute you could see out the front, though poorly. "It's not far," he said.

"The scraper," Uncle Hersh insisted. "You'll run someone over." He got out of the car and walked around to the front. "Your headlights are covered up."

"Use your undershirt."

"The scraper, Bert. Give it to me."

"Get back in the car," the Congressman yelled. "Everybody's freezing."

In the blurred beam of the headlights we could all see Uncle Hersh shake his fist. Then he kicked the front bumper. "The scraper," he yelled furiously, throwing his arms into the air. His breath was visible in the cold and you could tell from the puffs that he was panting. "Get back in the car," shouted the Congressman. Then he leaned on the horn.

Uncle Hersh pulled off his topcoat and threw it down in the snow. He tore open his jacket. He grabbed his shirt and pulled, and you could see the buttons popping. He grabbed his undershirt at the neckline and yanked downward, and in a minute he was stamping around the car with the shredded undershirt in his hand. He wiped off the headlights, the taillights, all the windows. Then he picked up his topcoat and walked home, walking in the road the whole way. He wouldn't get in the car and he wouldn't let the car pass. We followed him through the snow and nobody said a word.

He didn't die from that, especially. But it wasn't many months more. We brought him to the cemetery in New Jersey where his parents are buried. New England Turnpike, Cross Bronx Expressway, George Washington Bridge. The fastest.

Aunt Florence lives in Mexico City now. She has good friends and good health. She sends us gifts of leather and silver and jade, always nice though inexpensive.

Senator, formerly Congressman, Dvorsky is in his second term. There's talk that he may go higher still—the first Jewish Vice President. We're on his Christmas card list and we both get cards on our birthdays. He'd do us favors, but forget the favors.

Janet and I are married. We cheat very little on our tax

returns. We're still trying to have a child. Sometimes she dreams about Uncle Hersh. In the morning she tells me, "He was here for dinner. He said he'd been away in a hospital but now he's all right. He looked the same." Then she screws up her eyes and forehead, something she does too much. I want to see her lying on the beach, stretched out and relaxed, turning brown in the sun, but these days we live hundreds of miles from the water.

# Things To Be Thrown Away

THIS IS THE SHELL OF A HORSESHOE crab. It came from near here, some May or June—the season they hit our beaches, coupling in the shallow water, spawning in mud, often getting stranded by the withdrawing tide. My father and mother brought Howard and me to see them.

Most that we found high on the beach were still alive, helpless on their backs. My father and Howard lifted the great horny things by their tails: the ten legs wiggling wildly in air, the abdominal gills flapping and rippling in such desperate thirst that I ran to my mother. She lifted me by my armpits. Leave them, I yelled, but they carried them down to the water, holding them away from their bodies at rigid arm's length. You're heartless, Adam, shouted my father. They swung them in with smacking plops, Howard jumping back to avoid the splashes. The beach stank, and I thought this shell would fill the basement with it—the dust must seal it up.

We walked by the water at low tide and saw them gliding, searching for mates. Look, said my mother, pointing: a couple, the male hooked to the larger female, scudding across the bottom. We kept pace along the shore. From those hideous lovers there sometimes arose a milky cloud of tiny bubbles. When they swerved away from us, my mad father galloped into the sea, trying to herd them toward shore, stamping out glistening sheets of spray, and Howard backed higher up the beach. He has always been cautious, extremely cautious, about getting wet.

Always, at the pediatrician's, it was I, the younger brother, who sat first on the examining table, legs dangling, holding the kidney-shaped pan against my neck, so Dr. Zorn could shoot an amazing invasion of warm water into my ear. That feels nice, I would announce, as they all expected me to.

Adam says it's nice, Howard, my mother said, reaching around to stroke behind her at the level of his head. Howard was silent. He peered and cringed. See how gentle Dr. Zorn is being? she asked him. Now the other one, said Dr. Zorn, meaning ear. Transferring the sloshing pan, I dropped a casual glance to it: practically nothing. If Howard envied my courage now—and he never said so, if he did—I would envy him in a few minutes, as he sat with eyes screwed shut, a thin whimper escaping his grinning mouth, while great clots of wax were flushed from him. To be so productive, so cleansed.

This stopwatch is from Woolworth's. Mornings, my father got his blood going by snapping his fingers until the sound was like firecrackers. Then he'd jog, so many times around the block that Howard and I would forget him as we played, and he seemed not to circle but simply to appear, like a tropical fish at the front of the tank. In summer he came back very red, and we flanked him where he flopped on the bottom step, elbows on spread knees, smelling hot and acrid as some process of heavy industry, dripping so much sweat onto the cracked cement walk that the big black ants of our neighborhood had to detour around the puddle.

And this too, this string of Ivy League pennants—we bought this at Woolworth's, too. For my father, who loved buying things, price was no object: a screwdriver with a magnetic tip, or a perfect hand of bananas, pleased him as much as a rich new suit of Harris tweed. Times when my mother wasn't with us, my father and I would rage through the store, calling to each other from aisle to aisle, fingering artificial flowers and student lamps and netlike bags of miniature candy bars, while Howard stood in the pet section as though tethered there, watching the fish swim in their silence. At the checkout counter my father and I would pile our pillage. Howard would have nothing, unless it was a card for our mother—he got them when Mother's Day or Valentine's Day had just gone by, at half price. I would try to explain the error in this. But on the ride home my father would nudge me and whisper, Have a heart, until I turned around and told my unhappy brother, riding in back with our purchases, that I was only jealous, his card was terrific. He would squint in doubt, wiping an already gleaming wrist across his nostrils.

This is a garden rake of very superior design. Nothing

like it in Woolworth's or anywhere: my father made them himself, down by the river in a tiny factory that he convinced his draft board was a defense plant. He drove his black box of a Hudson to real defense plants for hundreds of miles around, offering to subcontract, bringing home blueprints of weapons systems. These were marked CONFIDENTIAL and SECRET, and he loved to unroll them on our speckled linoleum floor and study them for hours, though he couldn't understand them in the least. Anyone who ran a defense plant didn't have to go to war. I called him a coward, but my mother and Howard disagreed. Some men won't march, she told me. Your father can't even dance with a partner. I thought she was wrong but maybe she was right, because when they found out that his factory was making garden rakes and not bombsights, as he'd claimed, he ran away, leaving us.

Our basement filled with garden rakes: our only asset, my mother said calmly. Howard blubbered. It's okay, I told him. We can sell those, they're top quality. My mother took me aside and said, Adam. I need you to help Howard, now. He doesn't understand things as quickly as you do.

This well-sealed box, which must be full of mildew anyway, is labeled DIPLOMAS, REPORT CARDS— H & A. By junior high school we were in the same grade, but how could I protect him? He'd stayed back two years. I had skipped a year and was practically a midget. If the bullies came after him I'd charge like crazy, but they were never impressed. Howard would let them do to him what they wanted, but if they came after me he would pull them off, and in a minute I would be running for a teacher while he lay quietly, pinned to the floor.

Dr. Zorn, who obviously liked our mother a lot, said I would grow, though maybe never very big. He said that for a mind like Howard's, none of the regular tests were valid, that Howard was probably just preoccupied with sex. If Howard was, he never said so. When pictures were passed around on the playground—pictures that I felt guilty and honored to hold in my hand—he'd frown over them the way he did over algebra problems. Yet he had hair, his voice had changed, and before I even had a wet dream he was masturbating every night, soaking so many Kleenex tissues that I would have felt intimidated if it had been anyone but Howard.

His genitals were well developed and would have been respected in the showers, where mine were ridiculed. But Howard, who hated getting wet, never showered even at home, and on Tuesdays and Thursdays came to our mother with ailments that might excuse him from gym. In this department Howard was gifted. His afflictions told the seasons: hay fever in spring, infected pores in summer, leaf mold allergy in fall, cracked and peeling fingertips in winter. Dr. Zorn thought gym class was exactly what Howard needed—gym had been fun for him, he told us, the trampoline especially. When he came to visit, he'd take miserable Howard into a room and shut the door to counsel him, but after exclamations that mounted in volume out he'd stalk, ruffling his hair. When I went in, Howard would be slumped in a chair, as limp as the freshly killed. Always, Dr. Zorn wrote the note that got Howard through the next few weeks.

When we were in high school, our mother got a judge to annul her marriage to our father. Then she married Dr. Zorn. I tried to understand why, and explained it to Howard as well as I could: she was lonely. It might be mostly Platonic. But Howard, who was sure that our father was still alive and would someday return, never forgave our mother until, I guess, the end of her life.

This bedpan, though I handled it then, is the one thing here I will not touch: this, and this shell of a horseshoe crab, maybe because they're shaped the same. I went to college, the state university—that was when I took down from my wall this string of Ivy League pennants—because Howard, who couldn't finish high school, was spending a year in the state training school, in the same town. At the start of the summer we came home and found our mother a skeleton, almost. Anybody could see what was coming. She hadn't wanted us to be distracted from our studies, Dr. Zorn explained. He looked exhausted from nursing her, and I envied him that. But my brother couldn't bear to be in her room.

At her funeral, I saw Howard looking over the small crowd, again and again, as if through sheer determination he could make our father be there. He even had me looking, making allowances for changes the years could have brought. Then the funeral was over. Howard was in tears, grinning, making sounds. I put my arms around him, and in a moment I was soaking. He was heaving violently, like a water-breather dragged into the air. His tears were stinging my eyes; he held me tighter and my ear grew wet. It's just us two, I said. We'll take care of each other. But he just stood there crying and gasping until I felt his tears on my neck, and I knew I had to push him away before the tide of him reached my heart.

# A Way of Life

THIS SUMMER, FOR THE FIRST TIME, I find that I can't take the subway or the bus. I lie here with my feet hanging over the end of the bed, and the shades drawn, thinking how even if you stay away from windows, and never eat a meal that wasn't prepared by you or your mother, your kidneys or something could go any day. I lie here sweating, a taste in my mouth like salted metal, hearing my mother at her typewriter—she's up near a hundred thousand by now—and my father working his seven-note phrase, and I put my hand on my chest, until I'm thinking about suicide, just to get it over with.

My parents are no help at all. Every hour she's awake and at home, my mother is working on a project intended to make her famous, get her listed in *The Book of Facts* and onto the Arthur Godfrey Show. Once she heard Arthur remark that nobody can count to a million, and she's proving him wrong by typing all the numbers out. My father, a composer of Jewish liturgical music, is the slave of a little melody that came to him in a dream when he was

*33*

seventeen—my age, though nothing like that has happened to me. He's giving his life to that seven-note phrase,
his signature, he calls it. For weeks he'll be pounding day
and night at his piano or his harpsichord. Then, when he's
away on trips, accompanying Cantor Korn in Miami or
Cincinnati or Boston, silence.

I'm always afraid he won't return, that he'll be stabbed
by some prostitute in a shabby hotel room. I'm certain that
prostitutes are his vice. Even when he's home I know he
goes to them, he and his buddy Dr. Leventhal. Mysterious
evenings come when he wears a scent and looks a little
pale, and tells my mother that he and Leventhal are going
to their chess club. She believes this, she hasn't any choice,
the truth would take her apart. As I imagine it, Leventhal
pays—he's got the dough, and often tells me in a loud
whisper how honored he is to associate with a man of my
father's genius.

My room is covered everywhere with dust. Each time I
roll over, it swirls in the plane of light that slides between
my curtains. I haven't vacuumed in weeks, and nobody else
ever does. I've been in charge of this apartment as long as I
can remember. When I needed somewhere to play, I'd have
to return the ginger ale and club soda empties lining our
hallway walls. When I could barely write, I was writing
checks for the rent, checks for the phone, the electric. If I
didn't, my mother and father would forget. How can I ever
commit suicide?

She's typing like crazy, seven strokes to the number,

including the comma. His melody is chasing itself in a fugue. My tongue tastes like it did when I studied trombone—he chose me that instrument because I was tall, even then. Then he left the hall in the middle of my first recital, stopping at the door to shake both fists at me—that's how bad I was. That's how devoted he was to his art.

My heart is pounding like someone buried alive in a coffin. The taste in my mouth has spread into my nose. I feel like I'm drowning in it but this will go away if I look at my bedside clock, at the second hand sweeping around so steadily. I slide my hand down into my pants and it's frightening, I swear I've never felt it so swollen. It's hammering with my pulse. I'm not seeing the clock any more—I focus again but can't hold it together.

I jump up and all I know is one thing, I am not going to lose my mind, I'm going to survive this. I am a person and someday I will be happy. I open my door, and in the kitchen the typing suddenly stops, the piano stops in the living room. In silence I walk up to my father—the brightness of the room makes me nearly shut my eyes—and tell him in a soft voice what it is I think I want.

When he and I go out after supper, my mother is already back typing, and she pretends not to hear me say good-bye. I look at her neck, the back of her head, as she leans away from me over the typewriter: nobody there. She's gone away into her high-stepping daddy longlegs fingers. We've told her we're going to a concert, but I know she's afraid it's a lie, and it's killing her. I won't agree to those shoulders. I'm ready to stay home.

But my father walks me to the corner, and there is Dr. Leventhal, it makes me sick to see him, puffing his cigar in the back of a taxi.

"Smoke bother you?" he asks, and stubs it halfway out, so that the crushed stump smells terrible. They sit on either side of me. "You're going to meet a blonde," says Leventhal, "trained many years as a gymnast, presently she's in secretarial school."

"Arnold, not now," my father tells him.

Leventhal is quiet a minute, grinding out his cigar a little more, squeezing its poison into the air. Then he says softly, "Such legs. All muscles and no joints. She puts them in any position you can imagine."

This makes me want to go right back. "Cut it out," my father says.

"I don't mean for you, Michael," says Leventhal, turning toward me, looking up at me. "Too sophisticated. But the *schwartze* is lovely, tall like yourself." Then my father changes the subject, and they talk about—it makes me feel completely crazy, sitting there listening to this—some dispute on the Program Committee at our temple.

When we get to the place, they take the elevator up and open the fire door for me when I come up the stairs, eleven floors. "You're sweating, big fella," says Leventhal, and reaches up to pat me dry. My father takes me by the elbow but I tell him, "I'm okay," and I brush away Leventhal's hanky. "Which door, damn it?" While we stand waiting, I can see that my father's composing in his mind. His fingers are stretching to form chords, then dancing like jackhammers. When we walk in, his hands are still floating at his sides.

It begins horribly. We sit around in a parlor, and Leventhal and my father argue loudly about which girl will be best for me. I wish I could cover the girls' ears while this is going on. But they only laugh and bring us drinks— Leventhal tells them club soda for the young man. They're dressed in leotards, and I can't look at them.

My girl is short and almost fat. We go into a bedroom, and as soon as we're naked the first thing she does is offer me a dish of M & M's. I take handfuls—at supper I was too nervous to eat, but now I'm starving, and I apologize for gobbling so many. "Michael, you're built like a Neanderthal," she says. She folds her arms, squeezing her breasts up at me. "A giant Neanderthal. Nobody ever told you that?"

When we start, I'm surprised at how our bodies fit together. It feels perfect for a second. Then I suddenly throw up and just manage to turn my face away from her. "Good boy," she says. She pushes me off and mops it up with towels. Then she cleans my face and asks if I want to try again.

"I don't think so," I tell her, but she begins to touch me and after a while we do. "You've got to move," she says. I close my eyes, pretending I'm back in my room, in the

dark. "No, no. With your hips," she says, and grabs my
buttocks. "Rhythm, rhythm," she says. My father's seven
notes begin to run back and forth in my mind. "That's
better. That's better," she says. "That's good."

Back in the parlor, my father is sleepy and Leventhal is
lighting a fresh cigar. It's shocking to see them there, two
men I've known my whole life. In the cab we're all silent
until Leventhal can't stand it anymore. "So?" he asks me.

I don't answer, I don't look at him. Blocks go by. *"Nu?"*
he demands, more urgently. And my father asks, "Michael,
you're all right?"

I don't answer, because I know they'll misunderstand.
Even if I'm glad I've done it, I'll never touch a woman like
that again. I'm already dying to be home and wash her off
me, her and the other men who've touched her, probably
including my father and Leventhal, and everyone *they've*
touched. And if I begin to talk about it, I know I'll say how
sick it makes me that, for my father, this is a way of life—
something this commercial and mechanical, something so
much against our nature.

They like it that I'm tall, they tell me, tall and with a
deep voice, because I'll command attention. My first job
after college is trouble-shooter for a bank. They give me
six months of training. Then I go to work resolving
customer complaints, talking on the phone for hours,
traveling to branches throughout the five boroughs.

I take elevators now, and can handle the subway except

when I have to stand in a crowded car. Then, looking down on the blind tops of people's heads, I feel exposed in front and in back, in the parts of my body I can't see.

And trouble-shooting turns out to be exactly what I've done all my life. Years of handling my parents' mixed-up affairs, of filling out their tax forms and making sure they get to the dentist, have prepared me well. I'm still taking my mother's typewriter in for repair—she's past the half-million mark, but slowing down, arthritis, says Leventhal—and getting my father's driver's license renewed, though I've never seen him drive.

My boss tells me I'm very good, too good for an entry-level job. She takes me to lunch a lot and we talk: I wonder if I'm in love with her. She's extremely smart, and always acts exactly as though she were pretty too, and I'm so impressed with her that I doubt she's wrong about anything.

But I'm amazed, and I admit suspicious, when Marsha proposes marriage. She's the complete opposite of me— totally self-confident. Our division is conservative, even for a bank, yet she comes to work in closely tailored pants that she's too hippy for. My hesitation causes trouble but she's shot bigger trouble than this. Her face is so mobile, she's got so many expressions, it's like an orchestra backing up her voice.

"We need each other," she says. That's something they teach you: showing people where their interests really lie. "I'm persistent and you're gorgeous," she says, and as soon as Marsha says anything, even about my own appearance that I've had all my life, it seems true. "We'll both be faithful," she says. She understands the way I feel about that. "I know how important your parents are, and I promise we'll live here as long as they do."

They like her okay. The first time she meets them, my father asks her, "What's your instrument," and it turns out, thank God, she once studied the French horn. We get an apartment on the West Side, close enough for me to walk over and make sure my parents have bread and coffee, and that the garbage isn't piled up under their sink. Marsha is afraid they're both suffering early senility. She can't believe it when I tell her they've always been exactly the same, including my father's vice—I reveal that before we get married, so she'll know what kind of inlaws she's getting, and can still back out if she wants to.

Finally, the night before our wedding, I admit to Marsha that I've done it once myself. At this point I can't blame her if she calls the whole thing off. But Marsha just takes my hand in her two little hands, and holds my head on her soft lap when I begin to cry. This is the moment, when I see what she can excuse in me, that I know she's right about our marrying, and that I'm going to love her the rest of my life.

She keeps her promise about staying in New York, but we don't remain with the bank. Marsha gets a terrific job running the credit operation of a chain of department stores. She brings me along; that's one of her conditions for accepting the offer. My own position is the same as before, trouble-shooter. But now I have to fly, because the stores are all over the country, and I'm terrified.

Marsha goes with me on the first trip, brings me to the airport many times after that, leads me up to the doorway of the plane as I walk with closed eyes. As long as I never see the plane's outside, not even a glimpse, she can get me on it. Boarding the return flight is harder; I focus on someone's back. The flight itself I don't mind, but the people in distant cities seem alien, so that I get panicky when the other passengers who've come with me from New York vanish into the airport crowds.

Later, lying in a hotel room, I see the interior of my parents' apartment, an object smashing through the window, the whole place boiling up in flames, my parents' hands combing the air as they suffocate in their bed. Then I have to telephone them, no matter what time it is in New York, or else call my wife, and ask her why I suffer so much.

"Because you know how to," Marsha says, "and they don't." We buy them an elaborate fire and burglar alarm system, and I feel a little safer. We start paying a cleaning woman to go in twice a week. I make certain she's old and ugly, hoping my father will leave her alone.

All along, Marsha's been saying that children are what I really need. She's right; as soon as our daughter is born, my parents fall into the distance, and farther still with the birth of our son. I work all day to save our firm's employees from their own mistakes, and at home I have these tiny soft clients whose helplessness I can't even think about. When it comes to my parents, my power of worry is all of a sudden not what it was.

My mother's typewriter has been broken for months, but it doesn't matter. Past 800,000, she's put down the project to go to work: a restaurant receptionist, age fifty-plus in low-cut gowns. Marsha says it's to punish me for deserting them; my mother insists they need the money, though we send them a check every month. My father now brings in very little. The temple has a new young organist, and Cantor Korn, who took him on tour so many years, is dead. My father's furious that I won't let him teach our children piano. But I don't want my kids to pick up my parents' influence; this is the only thing I ever fight with Marsha about. And something I don't tell even her: whether my father's senile or not, I wouldn't trust him alone in a room with my children, not for five minutes— not the girl and not the little boy.

As though to punish me for my inattention, my parents are aging with cruel rapidity. Marsha says this is perceptual: she's seen it coming cell by cell.

But until now I've been sure it was laziness that made my mother quit the restaurant. She spends all day in her bathrobe, flat on her back, most of the time half asleep, a movie star's autobiography or a box of Barton's chocolates riding her stomach or fallen to the floor. My father: however he ever was, I called it artistic temperament. Now I can see with my eyes that he's lost his interest in food and doesn't take care of his person. But is that so different from how he always was, the years he'd work day and night, between his piano and his desk, chasing some runaway idea? Yes, but don't I know he's given up playing almost entirely, and hasn't composed in years?

"Apathetic," says Dr. Leventhal sadly. He strokes a cigar, which looks unchanged from the Leventhal cigar of my boyhood, with fingers that now tremble alarmingly.

"Isn't there something," I ask him, "that you can do with drugs?"

"Naturally. I can make your father dance."

"So do it."

"I can order him stimulants. Or I can order him testosterone, which I'm the one who needs these days." He smiles sadly.

Now I remember, from my visit of last Sunday, how my father hardly cared that I was there, staring at nothing while I spoke with my wheezing mother, ignoring his coffee and the sweet rolls I'd brought. "He can still go on, can't he?"

"Your mother can't nurse him, you know."

"I hope you're not suggesting a home."

"No. I'll try what I can." Leventhal shakes his head confusedly, and for the first time in my life I feel toward him a grudging something good. I put my hand on his shoulder, now mostly jacket padding under the polyester, and he, faintly and dryly as a moth beating its wings, pats the back of my hand. "Genius," he says, "has a wonderfully delicate chemistry."

When I leave his office I feel relieved, glad to be sharing this with him. Some childhood instinct warns me that he's screwy and I shouldn't trust him, but I know I'm the screwy one, and I swear that for once in my life I'll be calm. But it's no good, in another hour it's cinching me up again, like an airplane seatbelt ratcheting tight under my lungs. So that night I get a sitter for the kids, and Marsha and I go to my parents' place.

And what's this? Here in the front hallway, waiting for them to buzz him in, Leventhal. Next to him, towering over him, is a high-heeled, high-hairdoed, black woman, a scented sculpture. An ermine-draped Amazon—her eyes are level with mine.

"She lives in the building," the old goat cries the second he sees me.

"This is off, forget it," I shout. "Go home, miss," and I reach for my wallet. But then the door buzzes, and Leventhal pulls her inside. We follow them down the hall to my parents' apartment: my father is there at the open door. He has combed his hair and shaved, and is wearing the red silk bathrobe I gave him for his last birthday. He looks already dead.

"Michael," he says with pleasure, misunderstanding the fact that we've all arrived at once. That's when I really know his mind is gone. "Come in, come in."

"He's a sick man," I tell Leventhal. "Don't shame him this way."

Now my mother appears in the doorway, panting, holding the door frame. "Bring him in here," she says, beckoning at me. Marsha is trying to move me away down the hall, telling me I'm going to hurt myself.

And that's when I see that my mother is in on it. She's giving me such a look, her eyes are holding me like arms, as though I'm the one, not her, who has to be protected from knowing.

My hands are full of polyester fabric and imitation fur. The hall is echoing with yelling. I see Leventhal and the woman staggering in front of me, back down the hall, out into the street. I smash her one and she hits the sidewalk, trying to keep her skirt pulled down. I pick her up, she's bleeding from the nose in red teardrops, and hit her again. Then Marsha is in my way. I look for Leventhal, who has vanished.

Back in the building it's perfectly quiet. But when I return to my parents' apartment door I hear the chain sliding into place, and, though I know I could break it with my shoulder, I feel locked out of my only home.

Now my father's in a home and doesn't know any of us. His face is all collapsed around his yellow teeth. His new doctor—Leventhal passed away last winter—says he hasn't any special disease, and says he'll probably die of that so be prepared.

My mother lives in our extra room. She's lost some

weight, and seems a little stronger. Last month she finished typing up to a million, but now she doesn't care about the *Guinness Book of World Records,* or going on TV. She says Johnny Carson isn't half the person that Godfrey was. The sheets of numbers lie next to her bed in shopping bags, and will be the last I have of her.

She's the only one who still visits my father—it makes no difference to him, and that's the way she wants it. It's not right, she says, for people to see him like this, with his mind gone. Even his own son? Especially, she says. All I have is his music—one or two recordings, some publications, stacks of manuscripts, and a seven-note melody that I still play in my mind to help me fall asleep.

Things are a lot easier now. For a while, Marsha was having an extramarital affair, but she stopped when I found out. She's had a big promotion, and now she's in line for Vice President for Corporate Finance. Our girl already has little boy friends and we've worked to teach her self-respect. Our son is the one who worries me more. He's good at sports, but with people he's shy. He's going to be tall, like me.

Lately I've had to travel more, and my fear is down to almost nothing. By now I've stayed so many times at the same businessmen's hotels that I can usually forget I'm in L.A. or Houston or St. Louis. I've got certain tables where I sit in each of the hotel restaurants, and most of the staff know me, if not by name then by my height.

But something strange, which seems to be getting

worse: wherever I go, the hookers are turned out like they knew I was coming. They walk past me on the street. They smile. I can't stop at a corner, or to look in the window of a store, without being approached. It's the smell of them, when they get too close, that brings me back to my parents' hallway, and old Leventhal bringing that angel of death to my exhausted father. I walk away but they follow me, down the sidewalk, sometimes right to the doorway of my hotel—whispering that I'm a handsome-looking man, asking me if I'm lonesome, asking me if I'm here in town alone.

# Frankenstein Meets the Ant People

THEY LAY CURLED IN THEIR CHAISE longues; the ocean foamed at the island dunes like milk. Perry and his wife were sharing a cottage with another couple. On the darkest nights, when the island seemed to slip its moorings, he sometimes liked to tell about his father and Jasmine.

He had been twelve, he could remember this distinctly. His father had come home on a Friday, impatiently fingered through the mail, lit a burner under the waiting potatoes that Mrs. Lawrence always peeled and sliced, mixed mayonnaise into the carrots that Mrs. Lawrence invariably shredded, and asked—he'd been a widower since Perry was two—"What would you think of my getting married?"

But the question was how Perry, a shrimp with an old man's cane and built-up shoe, no brother or sister, no money or lawyer, no understanding of guns, could prevent it. The woman would share his father's bedroom, where Perry would have to knock before entering. He could foresee the complete loss of his own privacy, and a shortage of closet space. In his own closet were collections and toys not touched for years, things that would seem babyish today, lifted out into the light.

"Who to," he asked.

For a long time his father had dated a woman like those in movie previews—that was how Perry still thought of them, because the movies themselves, his father had said, would be dull as hell for them both. The woman was thin, with huge mobile eyes, the whites too large for the irises, the irises too small for the pupils. Her perfume was stupefying, and she gave Perry stale sticks of gum from her purse when his father wasn't looking. When his father took him to baseball games she often came too, cheered at the wrong times, and incited Perry to plead for a cupped slush both of them loved, one that (his father shouted) destroyed the teeth, then the jaw.

But the woman whose name his father now pronounced, as neutrally as the time of day—"Jasmine Cook"—a partner in his architectural firm, didn't chew gum and couldn't possibly have ever cheered at anything. Her eyes were dead as marbles. All her expression was in her dark abundant hair, on which she must have spent half her life, transforming herself every day or two: poodles and ponytails, bunches and bangs, severe parts and sumptuous waves.

Vanity? Boredom? An architect's hobby? You'd see her head chained in braids, which it seemed to burst overnight, appearing the next morning in shock waves of fluff. For years, Perry hadn't understood that her manifestations were all of one person. She looked built to the scale of his father, the biggest guy in line at any ticket window. Her skin was so unblemished that it seemed to have just come from the store. Except for her unpredictable hair, she might have been a newly bought refrigerator, and it was that, her seeming not human, that always made Perry feel creepy after he had seen her.

"I don't know," he said.

Now his father was sprinkling paprika on the four chicken breasts, eaten five nights a week and endlessly reincarnated, that Mrs. Lawrence eternally skinned. In two minutes his father would turn on the radio for five minutes of six o'clock news. Then they would both sit at the kitchen table, reading, eating applesauce, while the potatoes boiled and the chicken filled the house with its sharpening aroma. Nothing would be the same: Perry felt a suffocating rage.

"I don't think you should," he said. Then he turned his chair around, away from the table, and sat squeezing both his soft upper arms. He knew that his father knew he was crying, but that they could continue the conversation as long as his father didn't see his face. If that happened he would find himself swinging through the air onto his father's lap, held between his father's arms and beating chest, inhaling the smell of his father's clothes and body; and if *that* happened he wouldn't be sure why he was crying, or whether he could stop.

His trouble, he would say in years to come, out for napoleons after the movies, masked and perspiring at

Halloween parties—his trouble, he explained at poolside barbecues, standing chest-deep with a can of beer (he barely swam but loved the weightlessness)—his trouble had been that he never had a plan, because even thinking about Jasmine hurt so much he had to stop.

The Saturday after his father told him, Jasmine came over so they could all (said his father) discuss it reasonably. But none of them discussed anything. His father mowed the lawn at furious speed while Jasmine, her hair back in a kerchief, edged and swept the walks. Perry sat on the grass with his cane and radio and canteen of grape juice, now and then pulling weeds from the flowerbed border, feeling the house and lawn shift their loyalty from himself to her. When the mail came he hurried to get it—he didn't think he could even touch it if Jasmine touched it first. His father stopped and straightened, pressing both hands into the small of his back, arching so that his belly protruded in a way Perry found disgusting, then wrung out his sweatband and asked, "Anything good?"

And there was. The brown-wrapped box was marked KEEP FROM EXTREMES OF HEAT AND COLD. Perry took it inside and opened it at the kitchen table.

This was one of those times when the world surprised him with its fairness. It was months before that he'd ordered an Ant City from an illustrated ad in *Boy's Life* magazine, the drawing a closeup of two huge ants conversing in a cross-sectioned tunnel. Please Allow Six Weeks For Delivery—that seemed excessive, shameless, and he'd been pessimistic from the start, drawing less hope from the "Please" each time he reread the clipping. He came to sense the ant merchant's sneering triumph: here was a crippled twelve-year-old whose father didn't want ants anyway, the kind of kid you could do anything you wanted to.

But here was the package, and inside a manual— *Enjoying Your Ants*—and what looked like a little double windowpane, the space between its two glass panels halfway filled with sand—and a thumb-sized cardboard tube marked "LIVE ANTS!" His father and Jasmine had come into the kitchen behind him. "Lemonade?" his father asked, rattling ice from a tray of cubes. Jasmine pulled up a chair next to Perry's. He could smell her unfamiliar sweat, sweeter than his father's, somehow damper.

"How fascinating," she said.

Sweeping a dripping hand an inch above the swimming pool's surface, or, supine on webbed plaid plastic, thoughtfully patting his baking belly, Perry would try to convey to his listeners exactly how Jasmine talked. "How fascinating"—as though it were boring, and elementary, and sad. That was her only tone of voice, the pitch of defeated wisdom. No matter what she was saying, she said endurance was all there was.

She was turning rapidly through *Enjoying Your Ants*— even his father couldn't read that fast, and Perry guessed she was faking. "First drip some water into the city," she said. "May I help?" She brought the thing shaped like a double windowpane over to the sink, then back to the table. "Why don't I hold it," she said, "and you be the one to put them in."

"I'm not a four-year-old," said Perry.

"What?"

He began peeling off the tape that secured the cap of the tube. Of all times, he wished she were not here now, but with his father looming up at his other side, glugging and sighing at a tall glass of lemonade, there was nothing he could say. He pulled off the cap and peered inside—a slowly churning tangle of black. Excited, he gently began tapping them from the tube down into their waiting city.

There were far fewer than he had expected, no more than fifteen or twenty, but they were enormous ones, and Perry could see that this was going to be wonderful. They would always be in sight: their city was sliced so thin that their tunnels and rooms would have walls of glass. When the tube was empty he told Jasmine, "Put the top on." She reached to close the city. Then she made a peculiar sound, as though she had been suddenly squeezed.

A single ant had somehow not gone in and was clinging to the top rim of the city, its antennae twiddling the air. *"Wait,"* said Perry. But she was already coming down, her face averted as though the ant might jump at her. She caught him between the city and its top, and he hung out by one leg, his other legs working furiously. Perry grabbed the city, freed the ant, and dropped him in. The trapped leg detached itself and fell to the kitchen table.

"Hate them," Jasmine said, backing slowly away from the table, her hands spread like pitchforks against her thighs. Her face was still expressionless. Perry's father, wetting a fingertip, picked up the severed leg at once and took it outside, from where came the clang of the garbage can lid. "If you marry her," Perry screamed into the wall, but ended in humiliating silence—what could he even threaten?—stopped as suddenly as though his canetip had entered a crevasse.

"I want you at the wedding," said his father.

The ants milled slowly, apparently helpless, atop their sandwich of sand, and when Perry went to bed that night he expected to find them dead in the morning. But again, to his surprise and somehow his worry, the world was working as advertised. The little guys had gotten themselves organized and made a start on tunnel construction, piling what they excavated, so that the building went up as well as down.

"I want you at the wedding," said his father.

After that they did a lot of their work in the daytime, and Perry watched as the network of tunnels grew brilliantly, stupidly, intricate. The ants seemed to have no sense of how constricted they were, or how few. Did they think they could raise their young in those tunnels? *Enjoying Your Ants* said all of them were workers—shipping queens was against the law. How did they expect to reproduce, or what else were they building for? He fed them a cornflake every day, watered them, and waited for the first deaths: the dead, said *Enjoying Your Ants,* would be buried in a graveyard at the top of the city. But even Fiveleg—the only one Perry could identify—was hauling his grains of sand with what seemed inexhaustible vigor.

"I want you at the wedding," said his father. "Have some faith in me." He crossed his legs on the footrest of his reclining chair. "I've known her a long time. We work well together."

"Do you—" Perry attempted a knowing expression that a moment later he felt was ridiculous. Do you love her, he had thought he would ask, but the words seemed too silly.

Nevertheless his father understood. "Not like I love you. This is different."

"You haven't justified it, Dad."

His father looked at him closely. "I want you to be my best man." Then his father stared down at his huge slippered feet, pinching his cheeks with one hand so that his lips protruded. Finally he said, with an anger that startled Perry, "*If* it's a mistake I can *make* a mistake."

Perry felt unfairly beaten. How could you argue with something like that? "I won't live here," he said. Suddenly his life with his father seemed laminated into the past— even right now, stretched on the carpet next to the big chair, doing homework while his father rustled and snapped through newspapers, the smell of his father's socks coming through his cracked black slippers: strange! He wished he could tell his father what it was like— remembering the present.

("That's obscure," his wife would remind him years later, hearing the story again, with friends in a bar about to close—"Get to the car horns," she would tell him, stranded in a foreign airport.)

"I want you to be my best man," said his father. Perry saw himself in the wedding procession, walking alone in his great shoe, tilting over his cane. "I want you to hand me the ring."

Later, Jasmine came to his room, to see the ants, she said. Perry pointed to where their city stood on his dresser, next to his clock and Jacques Cousteau bathyscaphe. The bathyscaphe was a masterpiece—the only survivor from his years of building models. Now, seeing Jasmine's eyes flick past it, he knew he would throw it out as soon as she left the room.

"They're amazing," she said. "Why don't those tunnels collapse?" It sounded as though she wished they would.

"This is my room," said Perry.

Jasmine had begun to lower herself to the floor, but now she stood up straight, huger than ever next to Perry's little dresser, near his child-sized desk and chair. Her hair was styled like a helmet, as though she'd come from another planet. "Why don't you like me?" she asked, expressionless.

He would never be able to bear her as long as he lived, that was all he knew, no more than Jacques Cousteau could swim free of his brilliant chamber. "Because you're ugly."

"That's so." She seemed relieved, as though something hard had turned out to be simple. "When I was little, everyone thought so." And to Perry's amazement she began to clap her hands above her head, sidestepping around him in a little circle, while he rotated to watch her as she chanted: "Jasmine is a friend of mine, She resembles Frankenstein, I forget the something line, She resembles Frankenstein."

("Of course," said the girl who would soon become Perry's wife, as they lay through summer weekends in her vacationing parents' bed—"Of course," she said, stroking the hair back from his forehead, or kissing his foot that had never fully formed, "you knew it was yielding your father that you hated, not that poor lady." Jasmine had been something he loathed, not hated—a disfiguring illness— and though his heart was now quiet, the mark was there. Perry didn't reply, because he badly needed this girl. And in a minute she held his head against her breasts, or sat up in bed cross-legged, or brought fresh ice cubes for their coffee cups of wine, and asked him to tell her again.)

The morning of the wedding, while his father was out getting his hair cut, Perry stuffed some clothes into his school briefcase and caught a bus downtown. He had emptied his bank account the day before.

But at the Greyhound station, nauseous with diesel fumes, the throb of engines muttering from its tiled walls, all he did was sit on a bench ornate with obscenities, watching people depart and arrive. And it was as though Jasmine had infected everyone, because none of them looked human to him. Even children younger than himself—aliens in plastic skins.

Every few minutes a new bus delivered more, and others left. On one wall was a Greyhound route map like a vast anthill seen in cross-section. Perry saw how it was. The world was crawling with them.

He walked all the way home. The sun was high by the time he arrived. He wanted to be so tired he wouldn't think, but what he felt was only his regular walking pain and a terrible thirst.

At first he thought he'd mistaken the house. There were strange cars and a van in front. Inside, he found people in uniform: a fat woman in the kitchen, two waitresses setting out trays of half-dollar-sized sandwiches, and a white-jacketed bartender who quickly gave him a ginger ale. "Nice home," the bartender told him. "Those your ants? Pretty nifty setup."

"Your father was *sick*," said the fat woman, watching him gulp his ginger ale.

"Sick?"

"Just *sick*. I told him this is *his* day. Do you know he almost called it *off*? I told him absolutely *not*."

She bowled away back to the kitchen. The bartender,

looking after her, made one hand into a flapping, quacking jaw. Then he fixed another ginger ale, this time with cherries. Burping, Perry took it to his room. But now the room hardly seemed his, he'd thrown out so many things he couldn't bear for Jasmine to see—books with print that was childishly large, walkie-talkies with dead batteries, board games missing most of their cards, old snapshots of himself: in a sandbox, in a crib, riding on his father's back.

In later years a time came when Perry had to enter the hospital. He was to have tests for cancer, possibly an operation. While he was waiting to find out, his wife sat with him every day. Their friends from the city came, friends from the shore, until the room was like a florist's shop, and the nurses' aides laughed and brought more chairs, and people had to leave so new ones could sit, chewing each other's chocolates.

The man who shared his hospital room had no visitors at all. He could not speak; the doctors had taken his larynx. The cancer was still active in him. After visiting hours, when Perry's wife and friends had gone in a flurry of careful hugs, the mute loved for the curtains between their beds to be drawn back, and for Perry to talk. He lay on his side, listening, bright-eyed. It helped him go longer without his shot.

Perry told him the story of his father and Jasmine— how on the day of their wedding he had almost run away. How, coming home, he lay on his bed with the tingle of ginger ale in his nostrils, and realized, when he saw something move, that it was time to get rid of them, too.

He brought their city to his bed. Stretched on his stomach, his eyes inches from the glass, he watched their mindless scramble and rush. They couldn't know he existed, or even that they themselves did. And this, *Enjoying Your Ants* had claimed, was educational for the entire family. The ants knew nothing, Perry tried to explain— only what the whole world knew, the same imperative that held the oceans in their beds and hurled apart the stars. The mute, his cheek flat against his sheet, gave a horizontal nod. He was beginning to sweat.

At the end of the most remote tunnel an ant was lying still, and lay still as Perry continued to watch, even when he shook the city slightly. It was Fiveleg, apparently dead. Contrary to what *Enjoying Your Ants* had promised, he had not been removed to a cemetery. The other ants were just letting him lie there.

Perry had been expecting death—how long could these creatures continue?—and wasn't surprised that Fiveleg was the first to go. It was actually a relief. He got a tweezers from the bathroom and reached into the city, collapsing Fiveleg's tunnel, to pull him out and flush him away. Reaching into the air between the high hospital beds, he pantomimed the operation of tweezers, while the man with no larynx stared and nodded.

But Perry saw with horror that now, crushed in the grip of the tweezers, Fiveleg was spasmodically moving. "Reflex action," he explained to the mute, who crinkled his eyes in doubt. And in fact Perry wasn't sure that he hadn't killed Fiveleg himself, or even that the ant had been finally dead. He got rid of him in the toilet, then washed the tweezers and scrubbed his hands until they hurt.

Back at the city, he felt better to see that several others looked feeble. It was obviously time for them to go. He carried the city out to the back yard, to a spot that was mostly bare dirt, and dumped them. They wandered blindly, lost.

Church bells, he told the mute—who was now sopping with sweat, his hand wandering toward his call button in swimming gestures—the sudden pealing of bells was probably an invention of memory. But something had made him wonder whether he still had time to get to the church and hand his father the thin gold ring. He knew where the church was. He felt certain he could walk that far.

But he was still there in the back yard, retying his shoelaces, brushing dirt from the knees and seat of his pants, cleaning his hands and face at the garden hose and slicking down his hair, when he heard (to hear it again was why he liked to tell this story) the approaching joyous clamor of many cars blowing their horns.

# Emotion Recollected in Tranquillity

A FTER I GOT OUT OF THE SERVICE, I moved back in with my mother. Our temple was teaching contract bridge, and my mother drafted me as her partner, at least one generation younger than anybody else in the room. No matter which of us was declarer, my mother played the hand (her card sense was amazing, I give her that) while I sat behind the dummy.

Mrs. Leonard was another regular, a huge woman who always toadied up to my mother. I was the reason why. "Tell Philly," she'd beg my mother, as though we had food and she were starving, "to give Diane a little phone call." Then she'd squeeze my arm or sometimes, under the bridge table, always frightening me, my thigh. She was terrified her daughter would marry Richard Dean, a Gentile whose pharmacist uncle had been heard to pass anti-Semitic remarks.

"In addition to which," she would tell me sadly, taking me aside afterward during coffee and cake, "the boy is AC-DC."

Though this was close enough to the truth, I was silent

out of loyalty. Mrs. Leonard thought I hadn't understood. She narrowed her eyes. "Do I need to spell it out?" She puffed at her cigarette in the way she used to signal sophistication. "A switch-hitter."

What Mrs. Leonard didn't know was that Diane had been on my mind as far back as my memory went. I had felt for her, starting in kindergarten, an unforgettable hatred. Even then she was considered pretty, which I especially hated, because it drew attention to her, therefore to me. Back then, and through the first six grades, she and I were the only Jews in our class.

Diane was incredibly stupid, incredibly something— nobody minding the store, was how my mother put it. In class, teachers had to yell at her to pay attention. It was always the same. Her vagueness, her dreamy sweetness, made me want to hit her, but I was afraid to. And year after year, fat Mrs. Leonard, whenever we met, would reach out a hand to stroke my head, which I didn't dare lean away more than slightly. The smell of her sweat and perfume intoxicated me, and I watched in fascination as the flesh hanging from her upper arm swung like a water-filled balloon.

"Philly, let me take you home," she'd say. "You'll write a little poem for me." Her voice was so melodious, humorous, and inviting that I would nervously feel myself falling under her spell.

"You and Diane are some pair. A little bride and groom."

The idea of my marrying anyone was humiliating. When her mother maneuvered us face to face at temple "events," I stared at Diane expressionlessly, while she wore a simple-minded smile and tried to back away. At last she would escape to the temple's front steps and sit reading a book, whose title she would hide when she saw me looking at it, and I would join my friends in back of the building, humming rocks at the garbage cans with as vicious a sidearm whip as possible.

In high school, to her mother's despair, she hung around with a brotherhood of tough guys we all called—I never knew why—the Baldies. Their leader, Rodney Cooper, would take her to movies, and then, late at night, to a deserted golf course. Big Ones, he always called her, Big Ones, and she'd only smile. Her mother was right to worry. Loathsome as Rodney was, he made himself the love of her life. Maybe it was just his being the first: Diane was soft, and would have retained anyone's impress.

"Sucks and fucks," he claimed, standing with his friends on the baseball field, all of them smoking and strewing the ground with butts. "Shakespeare!" Seeing me on the fringe of the group, he drew me apart and put his arm over my shoulder. "Jew girls are the best," he told me, as a compliment. "Right, Shakespeare?" I imagined myself dividing his grinning face into diamonds by pushing it through the chain-link backstop, but in a fight he would have destroyed me.

Oh, she loved him. He didn't go to college, so she didn't—she enrolled in Hammersmith Secretarial School, whose billboard showed a giant hammer striking a door marked GOOD JOB, HI PAY. When Mrs. Leonard saw me at temple, escorting my mother to a bar mitzvah, she stared reproachfully. At the reception afterward she cornered us, holding out a paper napkin laden with rugaluch. "And you, Philly," she said bitterly. "What are your plans? Yale? Harvard? Brandeis?"

"I may go into the Army," I said.

She looked at my mother, who flushed but shrugged. Mrs. Leonard brightened. "A young man has time," she said, folding her napkin around the rugaluch and stuffing it into her pocketbook. "Are you still writing your lovely poems?"

"It's harder now."

"Explain to Mrs. Leonard about the Army," said my mother cruelly.

So I must have been able to explain my reasoning, then—I had to repeatedly, until the very day I left. But now don't ask me. It turned out I never wrote a poem about the Army. You see novels about the Army, but did you ever see a poem? They sent me to Germany—no poems about that, either. But once while I was there I got drunk and helped overturn some parked cars. And in jail I did write a poem, not about jail, but about Diane's face, which I remembered as too big, a pale floating target.

When I returned home she was working in a department store, going to the local college part-time. I enrolled there too. Rodney had gone to Texas to seek his fortune. Diane missed him badly, but was falling in love with someone new, the one her mother, squinting through cigarette smoke, called the switch-hitter, AC-DC.

This was unfair, but it was true that Richard Dean was (and God knows how Mrs. Leonard found out) a transvestite. Once a week or so he liked to go into the city dressed as a woman. Diane, who had taken to confiding in me (her oldest friend, she remarked sentimentally) about her love life, said it was the deception he liked. That and the whiff of danger.

"He knows he isn't a homo," she explained. Saying the word made her squirm. "He just likes to see if he can pass. Can you understand that a little?"

"Sure," I said, and I thought I could. "When I was small I liked to go around the house in my mother's heels."

Our temple had started a theater group, and my mother was there night after night for rehearsals. I usually stayed home alone. Though I met girls at college, they weren't right—that was all I would say whenever my mother raised the subject. To my surprise I'd turned out to be a serious, no, a gloomy person, and could hardly stand frivolity or even cheerfulness. Since getting out of the Army I'd had acceptances from a few literary magazines, and was starting to think about a book of poems. If I could accumulate forty I liked, I'd try for the Yale Younger Poets Award. That was enough to dream about.

But, as though I were forever back in jail in Germany, seeing her pale face float before me, I was disturbed to find myself—after all these years—contracting Diane like a kind of disease. I might have become infected in childhood. Like leprosy, its stain could have taken decades to surface. In any case, the way Richard Dean would slide his hand around under her armpit—as though he were sticking it between two cushions—made me furious.

It was Diane's cowlike submissiveness to him that bothered me most. She was pitifully afraid of his leaving her, already afraid—something I could hardly believe, in such a luscious girl—of being single all her life, and alone in her old age. "If I looked younger," she said (she wasn't yet twenty-five), craning to peer in my car's rear-view mirror, stretching her face with her fingertips. Her sweater rode up, exposing an inch of white back.

Finally Richard told her she shouldn't talk to me so much. That amazed Diane.

"It's natural," I said, because I could understand his jealousy. Sometimes, after rehearsals, my mother was spending the night with her theater group's director, a retired actor. It wasn't the same, but upsetting enough. "I'd be nervous too," I said, "in Richard's position."

"You wouldn't if I were your girl," said Diane—protesting her loyalty to him, and not hinting at anything at all.

Her mindless subservience made me angry enough to think she was right, he was certain to leave her—who could be happy with her for long? But at night, waiting to fall asleep, I had visions of Richard Dean dying in a car accident—sometimes my mother was in the car too—visions so clear that I frightened myself, and beamed into my pillow the thought that I didn't mean it.

At other times I imagined myself catching him in a homosexual act, and beating him up in spite of his being dressed as a woman, and telling him never to see Diane again. But I knew I would never lift a finger to him. He said he was a karate expert, and once, in a sudden rage, had half-squatted into combat position, hands stiffened like hatchets. "I can break twelve of your bones in two seconds," he told me softly. I laughed and backed away. Though the Army had tried teaching me a little of that, I had failed to learn it. In a fight he would demolish me.

Ghazir—he was a Christian Lebanese, raised in France, but an Arab was all Mrs. Leonard ever saw—was twenty years older than we were, with enormous shoulders and a walrus mustache. Divorced, he lived in a cottage he had built out in the country. Less than a month after she met him, Diane was living with him.

What, she asked me with a hopeless little smile, could she tell her mother? I didn't know. When Mrs. Leonard saw me in the supermarket, she rose from the freezer bin, a quart of ice cream in each hand. "Philly," she said distractedly, pointing at me with one of the quarts, the pendulous flesh of her arm swaying, the look on her face telling the world—while I pretended not to see, hurrying to the checkout—that I, my stubbornness, disloyalty, unmanliness, was the cause of it all.

I guess there are periods in everyone's life, like childhood, that seem to last forever, but when you look back at them later they're collapsed as flat as packing cartons, and everything's squashed together. That's what it started to be like for me now. Diane lived with Ghazir and finally married him. I got a job distributing newspapers, and didn't win the Yale Younger Poets Award. I began to send my book of poems to little presses named after things like planets and trees. Diane and Ghazir fought, were divorced, but continued to live together—their trouble was her fault, she was too demanding, she told me. Mrs. Leonard died. I wept at her funeral, but when I saw Richard Dean there, crying too, a guy who knew she'd hated him, I dried right up. My mother, svelte leading lady, was there with her boy friend, the director of the Temple B'Nai Israel Players. "The weight this woman carried," said my mother, "she's got no kick coming."

Ghazir began to beat Diane. When I, drunk, tried to return the favor, he hugged me until one of my ribs cracked. I paid to have my book of poems published, and stacked the boxed copies in my bedroom. Ghazir was seeing other women, blaming Diane, who agreed that she was driving him crazy, she wanted so much to remarry him. My mother married her director, they bought a condo in

Miami, and she gave me a hug and sold the house out from under me. "This is my chance for happiness," she explained. "Not so many years are left. What about you?" She made claws in the air. "When are you going to grab hold?"

I moved, then, to a furnished room near the university. My landlord was an old man who swept his sidewalk with painful care early each morning. He was completely deaf. I communicated with him in writing, but seldom, because my childish script irritated him. On a ledge in the dim downstairs hall, beside the disconnected telephone, lay a tract titled "What to Do in Time of Sorrow." It lay there, slowly growing a skin of dust, the three years I lived in that house.

Ghazir had been having an affair with a French girl who lived with a wealthy family as baby-sitter. She met him at his cottage, often bringing the children, when Diane was at work. Diane knew about it. Ghazir vehemently denied that anything sexual was going on. But when the girl returned to France he was broken-hearted, and wept with his face pressed into Diane's lap, she told me. Then he said he was going to Europe.

His picture postcards arrived with decreasing frequency, with no return address and no mention of his coming back. Diane still lived at the cottage, where, every time I visited her, she would talk to me for hours about nothing but Ghazir. The surrounding vegetation grew wild. I attacked it with a sickle. Winter came, and Ghazir wrote that he was working in a bicycle shop, thinking of getting married. He had asked his cousin to look into selling the cottage.

And a sign, FOR SALE, did appear, hammered through the snow into the frozen ground. No buyers came. Ghazir stopped writing. The cold wind oozed in; each time I visited I tacked up more cardboard. I left my deaf old man and slept in Diane's front room. Evenings, we made a fire and talked about our childhood, which she, to my amazement, remembered as perfect. Spring came early. I pounded open the windows, bruising the heel of my palm, and patched the torn screens. On a night with a full moon and a scented breeze, Diane and I became lovers. As we lay together in the valley of Ghazir's mattress, as she slept in my arms, I beamed a promise into her damp forehead: to compensate her for every insult and betrayal.

We moved back to town, which had grown disturbingly since we were children, and rented a garden apartment in what I remembered as empty marshland. I got a job at an aerospace plant—it had to do with missile nosecones, they said, but I never learned how. I emptied boxes of head-sized plastic hunks into a hopper atop a machine. They came out at the bottom fist-sized, warm, and smelling like model airplane glue. Diane, who was working as a secretary at the telephone company, joined their Executive-in-Training Program. We bought chairs and a sofa, rough-hewn wood slung with leather, the style that year. New sets of everything that came in sets—linens, pots and pans, china, glasses, silverware. It was the nicest place I ever lived in.

Except when we were at our jobs, we were together, even if I was just taking a ten-minute trip to the drug store. "You don't think I'm too clingy?" she asked.

"I love it," I told her. "Don't use that word."

Diane knew from the start how badly I was going to fail her, and her difficult job was to teach me that. She started practically at once asking whether she disappointed me, whether I was upset with her, as though I were a doctor withholding news of fatal illness.

"You look nervous," she'd say, or "You look unhappy," when I wasn't aware of feeling those things. If I did tell her something was bothering me, a backache, or something from work, she was more upset than I was, as though the trouble were her fault. She saw things in my expression that I never meant to be there. She heard them in my voice. She heard them in my silence.

And at last it became maddening, when I had been thinking about something, to look up and see her little smile of guilty fear. "I wasn't being cold," I'd shout, before she had a chance to say it.

But now I began to criticize everything about her. I said she spent too much on clothes—her dresses filled her closet and half of mine, many more than my mother had owned.

"That's because she threw them out whenever the style

changed," said Diane. And it was true, I had been unfair, most of Diane's clothes were old, I thought I could remember some from the days of Richard Dean—old and unflattering, tight around the stomach and rear. And how strangely somber. When I saw them by the dozen, packed together on hangers, I realized that she never wore anything vivid.

"You should try bright colors," I told her.

But she only looked worried and asked me, smiling a little, her voice as hopeless as though I'd suggested she leap the moon, "Do you think I should?"

Diane. I saw now that I was stuck with her, she with me, forever. We weren't unhappy. I shouted, but not often; she rarely cried. We bought a second car, used. She dyed her hair to conceal the white. I had an extra drink each evening. We bought a little outboard cruiser and moored it in the river. I hardly remembered, would barely have wanted, any other life.

And then one night—out for supper at Howard Johnson's—we saw someone who looked familiar. "It couldn't be," said Diane.

I doubted it too. But Rodney Cooper recognized us at once, grinned, waved, and came to join us in our booth. "Shakespeare," he laughed, squeezing my hand. His face was deeply tanned, his hair silver, his wrinkles full of sly good humor. He was just back for a visit, he said—he came every year to see his family. He'd done, oh, pretty well in Texas, had his own business, now. Contractor, laying pipe, starting to bid on some pretty big jobs. His lawyer and his accountant were both Jews, he told us, then grinned, showing us that he admired the sharpness and shadiness of our race. Diane, with an unconscious half-smile, was staring at him—trying to read his face, I knew, wondering what he was thinking of her. It was exactly the same as always. "Big Ones," said Rodney, as he reached for our checks, "I gotta ask. You two married, or what?" Diane and I shook our heads slowly, as though in time to the same music.

They live in Houston, now—I know from the postmark on their Christmas card. It's the same card every year, the one his secretary must mail to his customers and suppliers. The signature, Rodney and Diane Cooper, is in red Old English type, within a wreath of green holly. I wonder how many others come to our town, whether he sends them to his grade school teachers in their retirement, or any of the old Baldies.

The missile nosecone business hasn't been good. But by the time the layoffs came, I had enough seniority to bump a younger man in what we call the Publications Division. Now I edit and mostly write *Inner Space,* a weekly that's distributed throughout the plant. News about the company, contracts we've been awarded, results from the bowling league, necrology—the Director of Publications lets me do whatever I want. Lately I've tried some light verse. I don't sign it, but the other publications people know who wrote it, and they say it's not bad. One of them is a woman, Lila. She hasn't been to where I live, but someday I think I'll open Diane's old closet and show her the boxes full of my book of poems.

Last week I saw Ghazir. He must be close to seventy, now. But he still has his swagger, and I stopped on the sidewalk to watch him. He emerged from a barbershop, thin hair and great mustache beautifully trimmed, and jaywalked across the street. I wanted to stop him there in the middle of traffic and ask when he'd gotten back from France. I'd have liked to know what he thought of his ex-wife's marriage, whether it would last or whether we'd see Diane back in town one of these years, alone in her old age as she'd always predicted. I wished we could go to a bar together, he and I, and have some drinks and talk about our lives. But Ghazir was across the street now. He hopped into an idling Thunderbird, where a young woman had just slid from the driver's seat to make room for him, and drove away with his arm around her.

And when I saw that, I knew it was good I hadn't spoken to him. I might have told him that he'd never loved Diane, none of them had, that they'd ruined her. If we'd gone to that bar and had those drinks I'd probably have cried and said that I was the only one in the world who had tried to save her. If even a shadow of mockery crossed his face I might have grabbed his thick neck and squeezed. And it would have been the same as always—no matter how I fought, old as he was, he would have crucified me.

# At Center

"**Y**OUR FATHER REMAINS A HIGHLY sexy man," Bruce's mother said. She meant well, but it was preposterous, and he only stared at her. Like his father, he was fat.

At this point—it was a talk she had with him often—his mother might get crude. "Women like men with some meat on the behind," she would say, curling her fingers.

These reassurances deepened his misery. What did she know about it? On the other hand, Bruce believed that his father, who never said a word on the subject, understood his feelings exactly. Playing basketball on the outdoor court at his junior high school, he had sometimes seen his father's Buick go by slowly and sympathetically.

Still, he was surprised when one Saturday his father came downstairs in a brand-new pair of sneakers and suggested, "Let's go shoot some hoops. Maybe I can show you a few things." He was surprised, and dubious. He certainly couldn't imagine his father leaping and ballhandling like the pros, or even like some of the older kids he played with. They went to a park across town, where there would be nobody Bruce knew. The basketball courts lay baking in the sun. His father peeled off a sweatshirt: his T-shirt was tight and robin's egg blue. His stomach hung. The crests of his nipples protruded shamelessly.

"At center, Big Jack Bienstock," he said, and dribbled up to a basket. His shot bounced high off the backboard. He jogged after the ball with closed fists, his rear end bouncing, and Bruce saw that he had made a bad mistake in agreeing to come.

First, his father said, they would work on foul shots. "You stand so." He planted himself on the foul line, dangling the ball in front of his crotch. Suddenly he squatted. Then he straightened, threw up his arms, and the ball went flying over the backboard.

Bruce chased it. "That's the old-fashioned way," he yelled over his shoulder.

"What?"

But his father must have heard, because when Bruce returned with the ball he was frowning. He told Bruce, "This is the way the big men shoot."

"I'm not a big man."

"You will be."

This would be over soon. In fact, Bruce could pretend that it was over already, that he was smiling at the memory of himself practicing the absurd shot. His father, keeping up a line of encouraging chatter, retrieved the ball with hustle and snapped bounce passes back to him.

But in a few minutes his father sank to the asphalt,

winded. "Never smoke," he said. He wiped his forehead and stretched out at full length, like an earthworm after an all-night rain. When his breathing had eased he lit a cigarette.

Bruce practiced layups, starting his dribble from midcourt and driving as hard as he could for the basket to flip the ball gently up against the boards. He was missing more than he made. "Straight in," his father yelled. "Don't use the boards. Up and in."

"You're supposed to," Bruce said, knowing it would do no good.

"Like this." His father ground out his cigarette and slowly got up. Then he grimaced. He grabbed his right calf with both hands, hopping on his left foot.

Bruce came close, frightened. "What is it?"

"Cramp." His father sank back down to the asphalt, massaging his calf, rolling from side to side with his teeth bared.

When he could stand again he said, "That's it," and hobbled to the car. Bruce, anxious to get home and over to the junior high, ran ahead bouncing the ball, suddenly weaving his way to the hoop, grunting as he soared for a two-handed dunk.

But in the car his father said, "It's just as well we stopped. I'm having a little chest pain."

Bruce looked sideways. His father was hunched behind the steering wheel. "Did you have a heart attack?"

"Who knows?"

He hugged the basketball, breathing in its dusty rubbery smell. If his father died, he imagined, he and his mother would get a smaller car. She would call the Salvation Army to take away his father's clothes. His father's packed closet would be empty, dusty, and his mother would sleep alone. He wished he were someplace he could cry.

His mother was surprised to see them back so soon. His father told her, "I had a little chest pain, just a little." She glared at him, smacked Bruce's shoulder, then wheeled around without a word and grabbed the telephone.

Bruce came down from his room after the doctor had gone. His mother had begun to prepare supper. His father was sitting calmly at the kitchen table, a pillow behind the small of his back, reading the newspaper. "Are you okay?" Bruce asked.

"He couldn't tell for sure. He said I should rest, that's all."

"We'll eat early," said Bruce's mother. "Then Dad will lie down, and you can go out and play."

"He didn't think you should go to the hospital?"

"No. Don't worry, now," said his father. "Go wash up."

A half-hour later Bruce was outside again, bouncing his ball the three blocks to the junior high school. It was strange: he wanted to stay home. It would be his fault, he felt, if his father died while he was out playing. But with so little daylight left, and a game probably going on right now, his body took him to the schoolyard no matter what he wanted to do. When he could hear the players, each shout doubled as it rang off the brick building, he held the ball in his arms and ran. "Hey," he yelled, rounding the corner of the school. "Can I get in?"

Nobody answered, and he saw that he couldn't—it was already three against three. He didn't mind much. He often liked watching the good players more than he liked actually playing.

Little Madora was silky and fast. Madora didn't run, he sprang, and at every step his long brown hair flew wild. Then for a second he'd freeze like an animal, except that he'd toss his head once, and his hair would fall perfectly into place.

Paulie Pilner, the tallest, looked clumsy standing still. But he could melt every joint into the curve of his hook shot, as though the ball were a comet and he its tail. His jump shot began with an enormous bound, knees tucked up, so that he hung in mid-air high above the court until gravity pulled down the defender who had jumped with him, and then Paulie would release his high-arching shot.

Dick Brown's deadly jumper was the opposite, a beeline. And where Paulie was slow-motion, Dick was lightning: he was up and his shot was off and he was down again, already starting to follow in, while the man guarding him, seeing his mistake too late, was just beginning to rise in a useless leap. On the drive, Dick could break up his last step into a dozen fake moves, then get off his shot as though he were unguarded.

"Dick's a good guy," Bruce remarked to his friend Charley, who had just arrived and was sitting next to him, waiting for the next game.

"Dick's good," Charley agreed. "He taught me how to ass out."

Bruce was annoyed to hear that Dick had taught Charley. He said, "My father taught me some stuff today. He's not so bad."

"Like hell," Charley said indifferently. "That tub of lard?"

The game ended. Bruce and Charley were let in to play four-on-four, full court. Paulie Pilner's team, the losers, chose Charley, so Bruce got to be on Dick's team.

He had to guard Charley, which was hard. Charley was fast. "Hands up," Dick Brown coached. "Watch your man." Bruce tried, but playing full court he could never keep up. Bodies were flashing all around, and the shouting confused him. He stumbled after Charley, gasping. Somebody said, "Our ball," and he turned to head the other way. Then everyone leaped together, struggling in the air. He was spun outward from the center, lunged back in and was kicked and elbowed. The ball was free at his feet and he pawed at it but couldn't hold on. Charley slipped by him for an easy basket. "Asshole," someone muttered.

They hardly ever passed him the ball. He got to shoot only twice, two easy bunnies. The first time, Ernie Rich loomed up and blocked the ball, and the other team took it away on a fast break. Madora said, "Fucking kid eats it." The second time he went too far under, and the ball hit the rim on the way up, rebounding into his upturned face. The rest of the game he was snuffling blood, wiping until his forearm was red. "The kid's got guts," Dick Brown said.

To Bruce's surprise, his team won. He licked his lips where the blood had dried, swearing to himself that he would do better in the next game.

But as soon as it started he knew it was going to be even worse. Charley kept getting around him and scoring. Ernie Rich's little brother, Junior, knocked him down, and Bruce was sure it was deliberate. Both times he got hold of the ball he was called for traveling.

They were behind, within one bucket of losing, when Dick Brown called time out. "We need some hoops," he told his team in a huddle. He put his finger on Bruce's chest, which Bruce tried to tighten, hoping Dick wouldn't squeeze one of his plump breasts. "You basket-hang," Dick whispered.

They came out of the huddle and Bruce trotted the length of the court. "Well, well," said Madora, noticing. Then the other team took the ball downcourt, and Bruce was left all alone under the basket.

Squinting, he watched the play at the far end of the court, waiting for a pass to be launched his way. Madora was dribbling back and forth, looking for an opening. Suddenly he flashed by Ernie Rich, making him stumble into Paulie Pilner, and drove for the basket. But Dick leaped and got a fingertip on Madora's shot. He leaped again, beating Paulie for the rebound.

Then from the tangle of bodies Bruce saw the ball rise

and loop toward him, like a bomb released by the setting sun, and Dick's voice yelled, "Don't travel!" The pass was perfect. It took one bounce and settled into Bruce's arms. Everyone was running, streaming up the court toward him, Madora practically flying in the lead.

Don't travel, Bruce told himself, and struggled not to lift either foot from the asphalt. He picked out his spot on the backboard and locked his eyes there. But in the corner of his eye flashed Madora bearing down on him like a lynx, he wrenched his head around to look, and when he looked back his spot was gone. His muscles froze. At the last moment he managed, with a little lurch from the waist, to get the ball into the air, and Madora seemed to leap over his shoulder to slap it hard against the backboard, where it bounced off into Paulie Pilner's arms. Paulie flipped it downcourt to Charley, basket-hanging in turn, who banked it in. The game was over.

"Enough of this shit," Ernie Rich said.

Dick Brown looked at Bruce once. "Christ," he said softly.

Bruce tried not to meet anyone's eye. But Junior Rich walked up to him and stood so close their chests were touching. Dick said, "Fuck off, Junie."

"Aw Dick," Junie said. "It's a fair fight." He bumped Bruce.

But Ernie Rich said, "Shut up, you little shit," and grabbed his brother by the shoulder. "He ain't worth fighting."

Now Paulie had taken out cigarettes, and Dick said, "Gimme." Paulie offered the pack around. "Hey," said Junie, grabbing. His eyes lit. Bruce saw with amazement that Junie had forgotten all about fighting—he hadn't even been mad. "Let's go around back," Junie said. "If my old man drives by he'll cut off my nuts."

Paulie passed a lighter. Then they all walked, Bruce in the rear, around the corner of the school building, out of sight of the road. It was starting to get dark.

Bruce knew he should already be home—for the first time since he had come, he wondered how his father was. But he felt unable to leave while his disgrace was so fresh. They all settled down in the darkness, on the steps to the gym, everyone smoking but Charley and him. The cigarettes' glowing tips moved in arcs, dimmed and brightened. Bruce found a spot near Dick. The air was getting chilly, but the steps were still warm.

"She starts shaking," Paulie was saying.

"I'll give her something to shake," said Madora.

Bruce could tell they were talking about Linda Kent, the sexiest girl in the junior high. He didn't know her, but she was famous—she'd do anything, she couldn't control herself. When you kissed her she began to shake. Bruce had talked about her to younger boys, repeating what he'd heard, and by now she seemed like someone he knew very well.

"She starts shaking," Paulie said. "I haven't even done anything, and she's going ape."

"I'll give her an ape," said Madora.

"I'm kissing her," said Paulie, "and she's shaking and like rubbing her tits against me. Then she takes my hand and sticks it up under her sweater."

"Jesus," said Junie, rubbing his crotch. "What're they like?"

"They're like that." Paulie pantomimed the palming of two basketballs. "I can't hardly get my hands around them." He reached up, groping at the height Linda Kent's breasts would be if she were standing in front of them. Junie rubbed his crotch harder. His brother said, "Junie, don't be so disgusting, you little prick," and grabbed for Junie's hand. "Rape, rape!" Junie squealed.

Listening there in the growing dark, his legs angled so no one could see he had an erection, Bruce felt at the center of the universe. From the nearby woods came the mating song of hundreds of frogs, rebounding off the walls of the school until it came out of the dark from everywhere. Bruce felt as though the only real place in the world was where he was sitting, in a dim cloud of smoke from the glowing cigarettes. He breathed it in until he felt light-headed with serenity. "I slide my hand down," Paulie said, "and she's wet. She's like a furnace. She's creaming for me."

"So?" asked Dick. "You screw her?"

"You know it."

"My ass."

"Go ahead, ask her." Paulie sulked a moment. Then he

continued, "She's creaming for me. And she's shaking like all over. And she grabs my leg. And I've got this huge rod on."

"Jesus," said Junie, staring at Paulie's lean crotch.

"I've got this rod on. And she says Oh, Paulie, you're so *hard*. And she starts to rub it. Jesus." Paulie slipped a hand down the front of his pants to ease his position. Junie did the same. His brother raised a fist, and he hurriedly withdrew his hand.

"Then she says, Oh, Paulie, my pants are wet. And she takes them off. So I open her up and slip it in."

"My ass," said Dick.

"What's it like," asked Junie softly.

Paulie took a long drag at his cigarette. "Nosy little prick, aren't you."

"I'll give her a nosy little prick," said Madora. "Right in the old twateroo."

The cigarettes were burned down, and one by one they ground them out. Paulie handed around the pack again. Madora took one, and Ernie took two for himself and Junie. Even Charley took one. When the pack came to Dick Brown he held onto it for a minute. "Hey Paulie," he said. "How about if this kid gets one."

"Paulie, no," Junie whined.

"He'll puke his guts out," warned Madora, and then Bruce realized that it was himself they were talking about.

Paulie shrugged. "It don't make any difference to me. But not if the kid's gonna burn it."

"He'll inhale," Dick promised. He turned to Bruce. "You want to try it?" He held up the pack, flipped it from one hand to the other.

Bruce didn't. His father had stained, sick-looking fingers, panted when he climbed stairs, sometimes coughed until he was purple, and said it was smoking that had ruined him. "Sure," he said.

Dick handed him a cigarette. "Put it in your mouth and sort of draw through it," he said. "Easy, or it'll burn." He reached for Paulie's lighter.

Bruce was surprised at how slight the cigarette was. It had no substance at all, he could hardly feel it in his hand. But when he put it in his mouth it seemed huge, and he almost gagged. "You're drowning it," said Dick, and showed him how to hold it between his lips by the very tip. Then he struck the lighter. "Just draw easy." As the flame touched the cigarette, Bruce tightened his lips around its base and breathed in.

What he wasn't prepared for was the heat. He'd thought maybe he wouldn't like the taste, but had never imagined what was happening now: it was as though he'd swallowed flames. He staggered up, unable to breathe, the cigarette dropping from his lips, his eyes watering so he couldn't see. He took a few steps, still couldn't breathe, and sank to the pavement. It felt like a heart attack.

Then the night air was searing his lungs and throat, each breath making him cough as though his organs would come out his mouth. Someone sat him up and held his shoulders—it was Dick—and he heard Charley say, "Bru? Are you okay?"

"Fucking kid drags up half the cigarette," said Madora.

When he could, Bruce got up and walked away. He sat down by himself against the wall of the school, where the others' voices reached him unintelligibly. All he could see was the glow of their cigarettes, which might have been yards or miles in the distance.

The night was getting cold. He held his throat and shivered, waiting until he was well enough to go home without his parents' seeing he'd been smoking. The frogs, which had grown silent during his coughing, one by one took up their old song.

He hated himself for having hoped he could ever be like Dick or Paulie. He might never play basketball again, or touch a cigarette as long as he lived. No matter how his mother licked her lips and curled her fingers, no one would tell him, "Bruce, you're so hard," and touch him, any more than that could ever have happened to his father. He could picture his father as a boy, plump and short-winded—his father was what such boys became.

Now the glowing sparks were rising. They started to float away from him. He heard Charley call, "Bru?" He didn't answer. A minute more and the points of light were gone. Bruce sat in the unbroken dark, his back against the school building. A little wind came up, and the night grew colder.

He was still there, hours later, when a new and brighter

light appeared. It came around the corner of the school, its beam sweeping from side to side. "Thank God," said his father. "Are you all right?"

"You're supposed to be in bed," said Bruce. "How about your heart?"

"You're freezing, don't you know that?" His father warmed him for a minute against his soft stomach and chest. Then they walked home. His father took it slow and asked him to carry the flashlight. The frogs were trilling, filling the dark with their cry of urgent love.

# Investments

D AVID KAPLAN, A FREE-LANCE illustrator of thirty-six who lived in Greenwich Village, was practically the only person he knew who had never been in psychotherapy. Now, when he had almost decided to start, he feared he was making a mistake. No shrink could help with what worried him most: all his money was in the stock market, which had sunk to a new low and might collapse entirely—who could tell?

Not his stockbroker, Kaplan was sure. Steve, who was also his cousin, had tricked and bullied him when they were children. Once he had duped Kaplan into eating clay, moist pellets the size of jellybeans, warm from Steve's rolling palms. Often Kaplan could still taste it.

Whenever he mentioned this to his cousin, Steve grew furious, denying that anything like it had happened. Kaplan was crackers, he said, one hand jingling the coins in his pocket, his bald head shining aggressively. Kaplan needed to be shrunk, but *fast*. "My guy's terrific," Steve said. "See him for Barbara's sake, if you won't for your own." Steve's guy was Phil Traub.

Kaplan's mother, however, recommended a Dr. Del-Vecchio, who had worked wonders for her friends. "Edith Timmerman was climbing the walls," she said. "And now!" To suggest Edith's present relaxation, Kaplan's mother released a ball of cigarette smoke with a pop of her lips. Kaplan screwed up his eyes. She apologized. But the ball was already expanding, enveloping Kaplan as he flapped his hand at it.

His girl friend Jane—his first affair as a married man—was pushing for Frederika Grunwald, her own therapist for four years. "She can't shrink us both, can she?" Kaplan asked. "Whose side would she be on?"

But though he raised objections, he secretly welcomed all advice. If he was going to go into this at all (and he still had serious doubts), the important thing was to choose his doctor carefully.

It was for a Monday that he managed to set up the appointments. "I'll probably be all right," his wife said. Thoughtfully she felt her breastbone, like an item of produce perhaps too ripe. "Suppose I need to go to the hospital?"

"Isn't your painting group meeting here?" Barbara belonged to a circle of artists who shared a model once a week.

"I'll have to call that off." She peered at Kaplan. "You think I'm making it up?"

He shook his head. Ever since her heart attack, Barbara had been weak and floppy as a houseplant, and often terrified him by holding her chest and turning pale. "If you don't feel well," he said, "you should rest." The concern that he heard in his voice depressed him. It was as though he wanted to stay with her, today and forever.

"Your pity is a razor blade," she said.

"Don't start this, okay?"

"If I thought I could rely on the ambulance I wouldn't even ask you."

"What's this ambulance?"

"I can always call your mother." She turned away. Kaplan could see, through her thinning hair, the dead white of her scalp. "Go, David," she said. "Go."

His first appointment was at ten with Traub, who practiced high up in an old building west of Central Park. The chairs in Traub's office were covered with white Naugahyde, the Naugahyde with transparent plastic. Kaplan was revolted and sat with difficulty. It was like the waiting room at his mother's beauty parlor.

When Kaplan said his life was succumbing to entropy, had lost its critical mass—when he told how his life seemed to be living him, rather than vice versa—Traub soon began making dismissive finger-flicks at the air, as though Kaplan's words hung there in a cartoonist's bubble. "I'd like some specifics," he said.

"Some particulars?"

"Specifics, particulars," Traub said indifferently.

Kaplan couldn't stand a quibbler. "Money," he said. "You mean like that?"

"Money," Traub agreed.

"My father's estate was in the six figures. Then I let my cousin Steve put me in new issues. Ham King? A franchise deal, trades on the fame of Hamilton King."

"Hamilton King?"

"I bought it at eleven. Sold it at eight. Then there was Medicomp."

"The baseball player?"

"Golfer," said Kaplan, annoyed. It seemed to him painfully affected for a man with these chairs not to know Hamilton King. "Medicomp we missed at issue. It came at fifteen, I caught it at seventeen, I was lucky to get out at twelve. What's left is in Protection Devices. Systems to prevent airplane hijacks? Steve touted it to me at six, I bought it at nine, now the bid price is three and an eighth." Across the room, a digital clock advanced to 10:16. "It's money."

"Money."

"Money."

"Specifics."

"One thing, I married unhappily. If I could afford the support, I'd leave Barbara."

"Why are you looking at the clock?"

"The market opened at ten."

"And your money may be trickling away." Traub dragged everything he could from the word: trick-a-ling. "How does that make you feel?"

Kaplan had a mental picture of his large bald cousin, cradling a telephone receiver between shoulder and ear while with delicate fingers he unwrapped a candy bar. "I'm sitting in Protection Devices, off two last week. Say now I call and ask Steve, Steve, shouldn't I get out. He'll tell me take it easy, take it easy, *bubby*, the big boys are driving out the weak money. Hang tough for Barbara's sake, if you can't for your own."

"And this makes you feel—"

"Agonized."

"I mean now." Traub frowned. "I don't believe you're feeling a thing. You own how many shares of Protection Devices?"

Kaplan saw that he could never work with Traub. "Fifteen thousand."

"So let's see. Last week you lost thirty thousand dollars."

"Okay, I should have sold right then. Steve talked me out of it."

"And how did you feel after you let him do that?"

Now Traub had pierced him. Kaplan pictured himself replacing the phone after that conversation with Steve, and the feeling he had had came gurgling up, a nauseous ruptured sensation. "This is absurd, sitting here talking about it. You'd sell, wouldn't you, Dr. Traub. I ought to be parked in treasury bills." He spotted the telephone. "Let me call, please."

Traub said nothing, but seemed amused. Kaplan guessed that Traub had written him off. Steve appeared to be away from his desk, said the switchboard girl. The

Dow? Off twelve. No, Kaplan said, Steve couldn't call him, he'd try later.

When he hung up he realized that he'd been cradling the phone to hide it from Traub, who was now standing. "I know," Kaplan said. "My fault. I felt negative the minute I walked in. Personal things like furnishings"—he shuddered and gathered himself in the chair—"shouldn't matter. It's my own fault, I'm an illustrator. My wife paints."

Traub was his. He stared at Kaplan for a long moment, then softly answered, "The taste is my wife's."

Kaplan's next appointment was with short, silver-haired DelVecchio, the kind of rugged little man who always made him want to confide. Water buffalo, Kaplan thought. "Barbara's clever, but cold," he said, looking around the room. "I'll admit this, she's been loyal." It was the paintings: swirling oils in thickly caked earth tones, slapped on with a putty knife. Cattle wallows. "Jane's spontaneous and warm, but I don't know whether to trust her."

As though exasperated, DelVecchio sighed. He sat behind a desk, which Kaplan had thought psychiatrists never did—a fussy desk—antique, richly carved, carelessly refinished.

"A younger man is after her," Kaplan said. "A fellow student, one Conrad. She says he's just an entertaining mind. I'm not sure what to think."

"You're not angry?" DelVecchio's eyebrows rose dramatically, as though he were acting out the word *astonished* in a game of charades.

"In a personal sense he's nothing to me."

"What sort of man wouldn't feel anger? How would you describe such a man?"

Kaplan shrugged. He had always liked being told what he was feeling, on which his mind was more open than he guessed it should be, but he was starting to feel disoriented. DelVecchio's manner suggested that he was not here with Kaplan alone. He spoke and gestured as though from a stage, making Kaplan suspect that this session was being videotaped. A shrink would relish that question.

"Or maybe," DelVecchio pursued, "you haven't invested much in Jane, despite what you're telling me. I want to hear more about your wife."

Kaplan said he'd get a divorce if he could afford one, and explained how Steve's advice had left him practically broke. "I decided this morning to sell out, but he's away from his desk while the market is collapsing."

"And toward him you feel—"

"Resentment, naturally."

"Resentment." DelVecchio screwed up his face in a pantomime of confusion. He scratched his head and shook it. "There's something I'm not getting here. Mere resentment?"

"You don't know Steve. His stupidity is a force of nature. You don't hate the weather."

DelVecchio nodded, satisfied, as though Kaplan's response nicely confirmed a pretty hypothesis. "We'll need to talk more about your cousin."

"I'd like to talk to him now," Kaplan said. "May I call?"

DelVecchio pushed his phone across the desk. But the word was that Steve had gone for the day. The Dow was off nineteen.

Kaplan slammed down the phone, shouting, "How can he leave in the middle of a panic? At this moment I could be wiped out."

DelVecchio tilted back and crossed his ankles on his desk. "What sort of man am I describing," he said, and began ticking points off on his fingers. "Despite lack of gratification, he helplessly orbits his invalided wife. Approaching forty, he's troubled by his hatred of his mother. He hasn't been able to manage his money or even rescue it from his dominant cousin. He's calm about the possible loss of his girl friend. He feels what? A genteel resentment." Dramatizing disbelief, DelVecchio half averted his face, pushing the heels of both palms toward Kaplan in a double stiff-arm. "I don't buy that."

Kaplan felt suddenly exhausted. "I'll never convince you," he said. "And you'll never convince me, the way you do those reactions. Why not say what you think? You've got the case all doped out."

DelVecchio's feet stayed on his desk. "As a matter of fact I have," he said. "First of all, the switch to a new libidinal object is a universal fantasy, someday they'll find a gene for it. As for investing, I like special-situation asset plays. But this is superficial. We don't change the world, we change ourselves." Now his feet came down and he leaned forward earnestly. "You've got to stop being so passive, just as I had to. Look." He tugged back a cuff. "Last night I repaired this watch myself. Notice the paintings?" He swept an arm through the air. "Mine. I refinished every piece in my home. And office." He rapped his knuckles on the desk.

Kaplan met Jane for lunch at Oscar's. She hadn't slept, and her headache was killing her. Jane's headaches were frequent. The more haggard she looked, the more touchingly lovely Kaplan thought her. He wondered whether at such times she reminded him of Barbara. Sometimes, sitting on the edge of Jane's bed, massaging her scalp, he felt the profoundest peace he had known in years.

But today his sorrow was for himself, and he resented her being in pain. Over the chowder, he told her that his hopes now rested with Frederika Grunwald.

"Freddy's brilliant, but she's not the good witch," Jane said. "It's not fair to expect a transformation."

"I don't expect that," Kaplain said, "and why are you protecting her?"

Jane scraped angrily at the bottom of her bowl.

"On this of all days, you should be protecting me."

"That's exactly what I'm doing."

Kaplan waved for the next course. The waiter removed their chowder bowls. "Let's say I asked you to come with me right now, take a taxi to the airport and fly somewhere and start a new life. Don't look that way, it isn't a test."

"I've never believed you wanted that."

"Would you?"

The fish arrived. Jane rubbed her temples. "David, don't make me do this. Can't you see how sick I feel?"

She looked so helpless that Kaplan couldn't beat down his tenderness. "Okay," he said gently. Jane looked relieved, and Kaplan realized with fear that he too felt relieved at letting it drop.

Jane accompanied him to the Yorkville apartment where Frederika Grunwald lived and worked. She begged two aspirin tablets from the psychoanalyst, a wattled dwarf neutered with age, and collapsed into a sagging loveseat in the waiting room. Kaplan followed Dr. Grunwald into the consulting room. A threadbare path crossed the Oriental carpet; the sofa's black leather was splitting with age. Grunwald herself looked frayed and poor, which disturbed Kaplan in view of her fee: seventy-five, this was costing him.

He sat on the lumpy sofa and smoothly, this third time, talked about himself. But when he was done she shook her head and said, "I had not quite understood. I couldn't treat anyone who is deeply involved with another of my patients."

"I told Jane that," Kaplan said, annoyed. "I knew you'd feel this way. Why did you even agree to see me?"

The old woman looked embarrassed. "I think I must apologize," she said.

"Jane didn't tell you that she and I are intimate?"

She said nothing, but shook her head slowly in reprimand of herself. Her dewlap swung.

"Then what has she been telling you," Kaplan demanded. He was beginning to feel dizzily weak, the way he had when he and Barbara, both sick with the flu, had tried to make love anyway. "Didn't she tell you that I was her lover? Or did she say her lover was Conrad?"

"Jane is a most attractive girl," the psychoanalyst said comfortingly. "I think all of us have been seduced a little."

Kaplan jumped up in a spasm of despair. "Dr. Grunwald," he said, "this has been very useful. I don't need psychotherapy at all. I know my problems, don't you think so? Now I have to—"

He hurried out to the waiting room, where Jane lay rigid on the floor, holding her head between spread fingers. "This is the worst one ever," she whispered. "This is agony."

Kaplan grabbed her by the arm. "Come on."

"You'll take me home?"

"To my house."

"No, this is killing me."

In the cab he howled at her, ignoring the driver's glances from his rear-view mirror. She shrank against her door and threatened to get out at the next light. Kaplan forced himself to fold his arms. "Freddy told me you and Conrad are lovers."

"Freddy didn't tell you that."

"You've always been a coward. This was your miserable way of ending it."

"He's just an entertaining mind, all right?"

The phrase failed to tranquilize Kaplan as it had in the

past. "Okay," he said. "I'm going to believe you. Here's what we'll do. You'll go home while I arrange things with Barbara. I'll tell her it's over and I'll convert everything to cash. Then you and I take off."

But Jane was slowly shaking her bowed head, her face hidden in her hands. "I can't let you do that," she said in a muffled voice.

"What's that supposed to mean," Kaplan said raggedly.

She looked up. Her wet eyes were brilliant. "David, you were wonderful to me. Right now I feel"—she searched for a comparison—"like your mother."

He understood, without any real surprise, that she was through with him. His first feeling was shame. Then, before he realized he was angry, he was swinging a backhand at her. She raised her pocketbook and he cracked his knuckles agonizingly on its metal buckle. "That's it, Jane, that's it," he shouted, until the words were only sound.

But by the time the cab turned onto his street, Kaplan was calmer. Though things were now bad he felt that he was getting to the bottom of them, ripping the last bandages from a rotten wound. He leaned forward, elbows on knees, fingers laced behind his neck, drawing breath and expelling it carefully.

When they pulled up in front of his brownstone, he could see people from Barbara's painting group at the windows of his second-floor apartment.

"So long," he told Jane.

"David, not like this," she pleaded. But he got out, paid

the driver, and gave him Jane's address. The cab pulled away.

Life, Kaplan realized, was brilliantly simple. He entered his building and climbed the stairs, one foot appearing before him as the other plunged away. It was just one moment that you perpetually had to endure. When he reached the top of the stairs, he found his apartment door open. The living room seemed crowded. In the doorway stood his mother, her face red and wet. Next to her was his cousin Steve.

"Where have you been?" his mother demanded.

"Getting sold out," Kaplan said bitterly. Then he told Steve, "You bastard. I needed you today. I wanted to liquidate."

"I'm sorry," Steve said. He grabbed Kaplan, hugged him, and began to weep. "I came here when your mother called."

Kaplan freed himself from Steve's arms. For a moment he watched their twisting faces, then rushed past them into his apartment. In the kitchen, a man was crouched before the open refrigerator. He stood and turned: it was the rabbi, holding a jar of something. Barbara's sister filled the hallway but Kaplan pushed past her, ran to the bedroom, ripped the bedding from the great empty bed. He flung it through the air, his nostrils dilating with Barbara's smell.

He was through. That was the only idea that came to Kaplan. There was nothing left in the world for him to worry about. They were staring at him from the bedroom doorway, and he stared back at them. "Okay," he said mildly. But moment by moment it seemed better than okay. Kaplan felt as relieved as a merchant escaping into bankruptcy. He was as grateful as a gambler in love with a crooked game, who is cleaned out at last, and can go home and sleep.

# Shrinkage

B Y LAST FALL, MY FRIEND DANNY WAS shouting that he was hot for the Mona Lisa. He'd become an art history major; her poster was over his bed. Yet he'd never seen her in Paris, and now ridiculed himself for having missed all of the culture, the two years he was in the Army in Europe.

His only stories of Europe seemed to be of village girls squirming onto his lap, of waking up drunk in ditches. "French girls," he told me—he had a high, powerful voice, like a trumpet in its upper register—"you perform!"

"Yeah?"

"Or they shrivel you."

"Yeah?"

"A German girl, that's the last thing she wants."

Though we were both seniors, Danny was older. His physical menace—in bars, I'd stare at the sculpted muscles of his hands—made me feel both nervous and protected. Now he wrote poetry, big Danny, and showed it to me because I was Editor of *The Breath*. It was flattering, then pathetic, and finally horrible, how readily he'd make whatever changes in his poems I suggested.

But that was typical: he relied on me in all kinds of ways, like finding jobs for us both last fall in the stockroom at Woolworth's. He made me feel like his protector—this bull, this ox, who could have killed me with one finger. We planned to work at Woolworth's till the end of school, and, after we graduated, travel through Europe together. This time he wanted to see all the famous paintings he'd missed, and I wanted to meet girls like he'd met.

It was obvious from the start that Woolworth's wasn't much of a job. The pay was parakeet pellets, Bud Gillette, the stockroom second-in-command, told me, standing with one pointed shoe on a carton of masking tape, while I waited to be interviewed. But there were some pluses, too, he said. He looked me over appraisingly, making me feel like a girl, and murmured, "You'll simply adore Siciliano," narrowing his lips as though he were afraid someone might read them.

I felt my own lips narrow in imitation. "Will I?"

"Sure you will," said Bud. "You like fruitcake?"

Mr. Siciliano, the stockroom boss, didn't have an office, only a frosted-plastic cubicle. As I entered, Bud and a lean, wheezing black named Lyman were sitting down outside with cigarettes and paper cups of coffee. They meant to hear every word. The walls of the cubicle stopped short of ceiling and floor, so that going in felt like entering a toilet stall.

Siciliano was doughy and bald, with baggy black pants cinched up tight under his belly—nothing fruity there that I could see. A pencil was cocked alertly behind his ear, but descended his veined temple as we talked. When it reached his eyebrow he would resettle it with an unconscious sweep of his hand. The cubicle was half filled by an enormous wreck of a couch, where I had no choice but to sit, and where, I was to learn, Siciliano lay every day after lunch, his bowels booming.

"This is part-time," he said warningly. "You know that."

"Yes sir," I said. "That's what I'm looking for." The ad had said two part-time positions.

"Now, Ward. You're in college." He said it as though he were informing me, as though I wouldn't know he'd just glanced over my application form. "Major English. You think you'll like the business world?"

"Very much, sir."

"I'll tell you one writer of English. Geoffrey Chaucer?" He looked at me searchingly. I gave a quick nod, telling him sure, who doesn't know Chaucer? "Geoffrey Chaucer," said Siciliano, "had quite a career in business. I guess you weren't aware of that."

I was, but agreed that I wasn't.

"That's okay." He was pleased.

"This is to help me through school," I said, though my parents were paying for college. I wanted the job because I'd never had a real one, and to save for Europe. I'd never been there except with my parents. I felt, in fact, that I'd never had any experience of my own at all.

"I shouldn't be telling you about Geoffrey Chaucer," he said, smiling painfully. "I never read anything Geoffrey Chaucer ever wrote."

He led me up and down the dim narrow aisles, between cardboard-box-filled metal shelves that reached nearly to the ceiling. "A lot of this you won't remember," he apologized. Then he proudly explained, in dizzying detail, what was where: hundreds of things, ashtrays and yarn, waste baskets and scatter rugs and nail polish remover, bird cages and three-ring notebook binders and curtains and clocks. He showed me how the freight elevator worked, and, to my embarrassment, summoned Lyman to show me the safe way to climb a ladder.

"Which is mostly what we do around here," Lyman wheezed, ascending with elaborate slowness. Siciliano thanked him politely. In a distant corner he told me, "Won't lift. It hurts his lungs. I try to keep him on the broom." He pointed out folding chairs and baking pans.

"Your ad mentioned two positions," I said. "I've got a buddy." Something told me to use that word.

"This side is toys. And this in here is all lamps."

We had arrived back at Siciliano's cubicle. Though I'd done no work, I was exhausted. Laboriously, in what looked like a child's handwriting, he curled a few words onto a notepad. I always feel sorry for people with bad writing, like people with defective speech—at the school I went to, penmanship was stressed. I felt they needed me here. Siciliano handed me the note, not even bothering to fold it. "You bring this to Mr. Beer-in-doll," he said, "in Personnel. He'll tell you the fringes. Let's see your buddy."

Bud and Lyman took me down in the freight elevator. "Well, that was the big S," Bud said dryly.

"Loved by all," Lyman added.

He was a juicy one, I saw that, but I didn't like their assuming that I was on their side. I knew they'd never be my friends, and they knew it. I can always tell.

"I thought he was gonna fart down at the end of an aisle," said Bud, "and you were gonna come shooting out like a cannonball."

"Covered with soot," said Lyman.

We had arrived at the basement, and Bud slid the door open. I couldn't help it, if this was going to seem real. "He's a fruitcake," I agreed.

Bud slid the door shut again. He and Lyman turned to me. I began to sweat. "Hey," said Bud. "You want to get laid tonight? Twenty dollars."

"We got vanilla and chocolate both."

I had no experience at that, either. "When my pay starts, I could."

Bud leered. He slid the door open. "Beer-in-doll's all the way at the back."

"Thanks, you guys," I answered, but it didn't sound like something stockboys said. Outside the door with Bjorndahl's name on it, Siciliano's note in my hand, I stopped, feeling proud just to be here, but wondering whether I'd make it through without Danny's help.

When I brought Danny in, Siciliano began nodding at once. You could see that Danny was made for physical labor—not just muscular, but so tough you could feel his hardness with your eye. Bud and Lyman disliked him, because he made no concessions to being a stockboy.

To my embarrassment, he was always wanting to discuss paintings—Pissaro, Toulouse-Lautrec—when Bud and Lyman were right there. Even when he and I were working alone in pet supplies or cookware, I knew his trumpeted exclamations reached everyone. Then I'd cut off the conversation and bring something down on the freight elevator. I'd hand-truck it back and forth across the noisy sales floor, passing and repassing the cosmetics counter.

Marie, the cosmetics salesgirl, was sharp-boned and hollow-cheeked, with skin the color of fluorescent light. Her hair, the luminous black of caviar, was long and thick enough to suggest that her wrist-like neck must tire—it made you want to rest her head against your collarbone. She wore a tiny gold cross and never smiled. "Inferior Modigliani," said Danny—he couldn't, he insisted, understand what I saw there. I thought about her so much it bored me, and sometimes, after seeing her, needed to go to the toilet and masturbate in what felt like fury.

Though I did no more than ask them her last name, Bud and Lyman were raucously amused. "Look at him playing pocket pool," Bud crowed, and Lyman added, as I quickly drew my hands out, "Let's see them. Let's smell them."

But Danny led me away and told me softly, "Marie's nothing. We'll meet girls in Spain that you'll never forget as long as you live." Madrid was going to be our first European city, because we were taking a Spanish class together, and so Danny could view, as we strolled through the Prado, room after room of Goya and Velasquez.

That afternoon, as the four of us were descending in the elevator to clock out, Bud stopped the car between floors. "Since Ward's so horny," he said, "maybe you guys want some tonight."

"Maybe," I heard myself say. "Where?"

"Maybe's for babies," Lyman said.

"Who's the girl?"

"Girl name June."

"Takes it anywhere," Bud added, his lips narrowed.

My head was full of Marie. I need this, I remember telling myself. "You're on," I said, and when I heard that phrase come from my mouth, and saw that nobody smiled, I guessed with surprise that I was really going to do it. "Where?"

"Here," Bud said.

I looked around the elevator.

"Siciliano's couch," he said.

It wasn't a joke, it wasn't a lie. They did it one or two nights each week, mostly for the truck drivers who delivered stock. Bud knew a girl and so did Lyman. There was an alley door.

"What about you," Bud asked Danny.

"Not me," he said.

"How come?"

"I consider it," he said, "childish."

And that night, in a bar, Danny convinced me not to go either. "Wait until we get to Europe," he said. "Think of yourself as an artist."

"I'm tired of waiting," I told him.

"It's too important. Don't waste it on this. If you've got to pump someone, pump Marie."

"She's Catholic."

"So go to church with her once." And he kept at me until, furious and relieved, I surrendered. If it was just to get my pipes cleaned, he insisted with mortifying volume, that would've been okay. But my first time? No.

I was afraid of what Bud and Lyman would say the next day. But they didn't seem angry that I hadn't shown. "I figured," Bud smirked. And Lyman added, looking serious, "Ward, you missed something real sweet."

"We got a special tonight," said Bud. "June and Barbara's putting on a show."

"Ten regular," Lyman said. "Cost you five."

"I'll come if I can," I told them, not intending to. But when I saw their knowing looks I swore to myself that this time I would.

I asked Danny to come with me, but he just gave me a pitying look. "All they do is lick each other," he explained. "You're throwing away good money."

So I went by myself. It was only what Danny had predicted, and there were four drunk truckers, clapping their hands and cheering, and something in the air that I hoped wasn't what vaginas smelled like. The girls were sweating and twisting and holding each other wide open. Their shaven crotches looked like something you find on the beach. The white girl was amazingly, colorfully bruised. The truckers sucked, kissed, cooed, cawed.

I left as soon as it was over and never went to see the girls again. But Bud and Lyman didn't let up. "You must know some fine young ladies," Lyman suggested, "down at the college."

"Get a girl," said Bud, grinning, his fillings flashing silver, "and it's twenty a night for you."

Staying out of it turned out to be harder than I expected. Some of the drivers who used the girls just assumed Danny and I were involved. They were friendly, gum-chewing guys, middle-aged before they were thirty, mostly Midwesterners, always offering you a cigarette or buying you a soda (which they called pop) from the soda machine. After they left, Bud and Lyman would mock their accent.

So it wasn't strange, one day while I was signing an invoice, to hear the driver who'd made the delivery tell me he'd be by that night. He asked me to tell Bud, and I said I would. "Take 'er easy," he said. Then he slid a ten into my hand. I mumbled thanks, but misunderstood what the money was for until I thought of counting the boxes he'd left me: eleven. Checking my copy of the invoice, I saw that I had signed for twelve.

That was the other thing Bud and Lyman were doing, and immediately it tempted me. Some of the truckers could get cash for things—I never knew that part of it, all I heard were the names "Singer" and "Floyd." If we signed for more than we'd received, the drivers would tip us out of what they got from Singer and Floyd, who knew where to sell the stuff at a profit—maybe even to Woolworth's again, but my guess was the discount houses on the outskirts of town.

Whatever stock we had on paper but not on the shelves wouldn't be discovered until inventory, when it would be charged off to shrinkage—a category including not only pilferage but also breakage, loss, low counts, expired shelf life, all kinds of things, and which no one would ever question, Bud said, unless it exceeded a certain percentage of gross sales. "You should be taking yours," he advised me. "You'll never get a raise from Siciliano."

"No lie," said Lyman.

"He's so cheap he rotates his shoelaces."

"He's so cheap he won't use toilet paper. Cleans his ass with a butter knife."

"You're missing out on everything around here," Bud said.

I told them I'd think about it, but I knew right away what my answer would be. Their concern for me was phony; they were safer with me in than out. But it was an experience I wanted, and Danny and I needed the money for Europe.

"There you go," said Bud. "Talk to your friend."

"If I do it so will he," I said.

But it was hard to persuade Danny, though I knew in the past he'd done worse than this. "How can we get caught?" I asked him.

"Right," said Danny. "Brilliant guys like us."

"Do you want to see those paintings at all?"

"I'll get there," he said, rubbing his fingertips together, his big head lowered, his eyes rolling up at me as though we were about to fight. "I'll send you postcards in prison."

"I'll be in Florence and you'll be here," I said, "reading art books." And when I said I was going to do it with or without him, he surrendered.

From then on our Europe savings grew quickly—some weeks our take from the truckers exceeded our paychecks. Final exams were approaching, and at school we were measured for caps and gowns. I decided, though I didn't tell him, that I would help with Danny's plane fare. At night, in bed, I imagined us walking up to the Louvre or the Tate or the Uffizi, in our mud-encrusted hiking boots, cheese and chocolate in our backpacks, hand in hand with girls whose beauty made me kiss my pillow.

But I'm the kind, I always was, who never really believe

that what they want most will happen. Sometimes I make myself not picture it, to avoid the jinx. But then I think suppose it doesn't happen anyway, and I won't have had even the thinking about it? And anyway, those are the ones I like best, the ones I guess won't really happen—ideas that come tinged with loss, like memories of someone dead.

One night in April, Bud called me at home. "The shit's hit the fan," he murmured, and I could tell, from the buzzing in his voice, how close to his mouth he was holding the receiver. The four of us had to meet. He named a bar.

I was shaking when I walked in, but Danny was there and seemed calm. I slid in next to him. The locks had already been changed, Bud told us. Siciliano was up in the stockroom right now, farting his way down the aisles with Woolworth investigators from the outside. "Who's got a genius idea?" he asked.

The silence that followed was unnatural, and I could tell that Bud and Lyman had already formed their plan. Lyman leaned back and grasped his chin as though in thought. "Say, Ward," he asked, "how old are you?"

I didn't catch on, but Danny said sharply, "Forget it."

"How old?"

"Twenty."

"Now hold on," Bud said, giving the air between him and Danny little placating pats. "Twenty years old, no record—the judge will kiss his ass."

Danny just folded his thick arms, and Bud turned to me,

saying, "Look at it this way, Ward. The four of us get sent up. Or you take it and get a slap on the wrist."

"Lighter than if you were part of a ring," said Lyman. "Which is what they'll call it."

And the strange thing was that they were right, I knew it immediately. I didn't care what happened to them, but Danny would get hurt worse than I would.

"All four," Danny said quietly. "We deny everything. Once they fire us, that'll be the end of it." And he stuck to that, though Bud and Lyman begged, until at last Danny and I left.

I should have known not to believe him. My parents' lawyer owns a sailboat with the prosecutor, and fixed it so I only had to make restitution and pay a fine. I planned to put the blame on Bud and Lyman, who'd gotten us into it. But in court, sitting with his head down, Danny looked like a genuine criminal, bigger and tougher than I'd ever seen him. All three of them got six months to a year. So this summer I've had the experience of touring Europe alone.

I walked through the Louvre until I got blisters, and stood in line five times to file past the Mona Lisa, trying to understand how Danny could like her better than Marie. I saw the Uffizi, and the Tate. As Danny had predicted, I did meet a girl in Madrid—in the Prado, in fact, in one of the Velasquez rooms. We went to bed and she shriveled me. And then I wished that Danny were there, so I could tell him Spanish girls were just like French, and he could explain to me the secret of the art.

Now the summer is over and I'm back in Madrid, waiting for my flight home. And what's really strange is how fast I'm losing all this. I already don't know why going to Europe was so important, or why I dreamed every night about Marie, or what made us steal from Woolworth's, or why Danny and I were friends. I have the experience, but it's funny—in a way I don't. It's only a painting: the two of us planning our summer, up in those tall rows of boxes. Danny's speaking, promising something, and I'm close enough to see where his shaver missed. But I'm up against one of those fat red velvet ropes, looped between brass stanchions, and I never quite hear the high trumpet of his voice.

# Temblor

SOON GREENBERG, CHEWING HIS LAST doughnut, stuffing the empty box under his seat, had passed the southmost billboards advertising Mexican automobile insurance—AAA, Seguridad, Sanborn's—passed them with scowling snorts, with jerks of his head, as though to indicate them to a companion—billboards were among the things he thought should be banned—and then he was easing his Ford Fairlane up to a dock at the San Ysidro border station.

This was the part he always found hardest, the waiting in line while uniformed Mexican officials let the cars past one at a time. Greenberg felt noticeable. Phosphorescent! He now weighed above three hundred, and had taken to smock-like monkish garments from a hippie boutique dreamy with incense. He knew how his face shone with sweat even in the air-conditioned car, felt his breathing grow short as some ga-ga pervert's. But today, as always, he was simply waved through when his turn came, and drove on cautiously into the jumble of Tijuana.

He stopped for a can of Coke and, double-parked,

tipped it down his throat in relief. Trucks were honking but he ignored them. Why did they let these dinosaurs fill the streets, which belonged to the people? Greenberg found trucks sensuous, their huge wheels and hot smell, but believed that they should be permitted to travel only at night. He leaned on his horn, then rolled the Coke can under his seat and pulled out into traffic.

The place specialized in muffler repair, and it stood at the end of a shabby dead-end street in a district of warehouses. Greenberg could have seesawed aloft three, maybe four, of the grease-stained proprietor, whose tiny size he felt as a kind of protest. This man (genes? nutrition?) admitted him by swinging a wide sagging door outward, then pulled it shut behind him. The interior of the garage was dimly lit by fluorescent bulbs grown woolly with dust. "Vicente's in back," said the mechanic, descending into a work pit underneath Greenberg's car, his hands filled with wrenches. "Bring him what you got." "Yeah, yeah," said Greenberg impatiently, but imagined himself climbing back into his car and smashing his way out.

Though his life now held serious risks—some would say danger, but the word embarrassed him—Greenberg accepted those risks. But this morning he had awakened in terror.

He lay rigid, his eyes darting about his bedroom. His clothes and shoes, which he had set out the night before, seemed cunning, as tense and motionless as a trap. The walls were barred with slats of sunlight. Stealthily he reached out to his bedside table and clicked off the whoosh of his Sleep-Mate.

The house was quiet except for the normal sounds of his wife and daughter at breakfast, and Greenberg gradually relaxed, until he felt safe in stretching his arms and legs. Though they had lived in San Diego for six years, the brilliance of the morning outside his louvered mini-shutters always seemed like a gift from God. Even a palm tree he didn't, like some, take for granted.

Puzzled, he examined his dread, and failed to account for it. Vicente; after that a house: his plans for the day worried him only normally. He and his wife had made love the night before last (the memory still good, he found, for a retrospective twitch and gasp); he felt confident that they would again soon. Maybe he was upset about his father, sick with the flu back in Cleveland. The old fart was failing, but what could Greenberg do? Bring him to San Diego, yes. If his father just once sat and watched what went into Greenberg's mouth, if he saw the time and guessed the money his son lost on horses and dogs, he'd have a stroke. That possibility, for some reason, had occupied Greenberg's imagination lately: his father twisting, purple, collapsed; himself applying mouth-to-mouth. But why would he be dreading that today?

He remembered the special on crime that he had made his family watch the evening before. Last year, a housebreaker had stolen all their wedding silver while they were just next door at the Katzes' for bridge. After that he'd slept with fear for weeks, almost like what he was feeling this morning. And even in this neighborhood there had been rapes. Greenberg's wife, a stockbroker, was rarely home by herself, and after so many years of marriage seemed too much his for anyone else to imagine touching. He worried more about his daughter, now starting high school—a round-eyed, baby-cheeked, tough-talking girl, just the sort that he was afraid a rapist might like. Smart-ass! Though he had once shouted at her, pleaded with her, for an entire evening, pacing before the sofa where she sat at ease in positions that looked excruciating, she told him he was rully too much and refused to carry a chemical deterrent in her pocketbook. Oh, she was asking for it. She was more than asking for it. She was practically begging for it. She was begging, period—what practically? It drove him wild.

Opening his trunk was always another bad part. Green-berg knew he had to expect that, and pushed down the surging feeling that it would happen now, whatever he'd awakened dreading. Vicente might have been caught, might have the Mexican police here with him. Greenberg could picture himself hauled away in a swarm of them to undergo interrogation, the rubber truncheon, electrodes taped—clipped?—sewn! to his nipples and genitals, and finally a cell where a vortex of flies arose from the shit-hole in the corner. "I want a lawyer," he whispered into the depths of his trunk. "I want to telephone my wife." Or

Vicente himself (whose cigar Greenberg could smell) might now be waiting to rob and stiletto him—Greenberg always thought about that. But he couldn't believe he believed it, because if he did he wouldn't be here.

Vicente, lounging in a swivel chair, lifted his cigar in silent greeting as Greenberg entered the garage office. On the metal desk before him lay a large, opened, but still full package of corn chips. "Am I late?" Greenberg asked.

Vicente spread a hand to deny it, or else to indicate only five minutes. He was as heavy as Greenberg, and bald, poor guy, but with curly hair on the backs of his hands, chest hair sprouting at his neckline. Tortuous veins crawled up both his temples. He lowered his feet from the desk to the floor, pushed the corn chips aside, and centered a pad and pencil in front of him. "You bring me some candy?"

Greenberg opened the flannel wrappings carefully. The things inside were individually folded in tissues; he had learned not to show Vicente everything at once. Vicente produced a jeweler's eyepiece and Greenberg slid him the first one, an engagement ring set with a small diamond. After a minute Vicente scribbled a figure on his pad, then held out his hand for the next item, a turquoise egg on a silver chain. Greenberg found himself salivating (the wisdom of the mouth—how slow the brain sometimes was—the way his wife learned from her secretions that she was ready for him—no, it was nothing like that) and reached toward the corn chips.

The total had passed two thousand dollars when they

came to the last packet, the largest. Greenberg unwrapped it with a flourish, and Vicente, though his expression didn't change, nodded. "India, maybe," he said. Two matching gold bracelets of what Greenberg now saw was Oriental workmanship, encrusted with turquoise, rubies, emeralds, sapphires. "Very nice," Vicente said.

Greenberg had known that these must be the finest pieces he'd ever handled. Some jeweler would get maybe thirty-forty thousand for them. "So make me an offer," he said, prepared to take eight, seven, even five—that would still make this his biggest day.

But Vicente was switching a strict finger from side to side. "I can't touch those."

"Why not?"

"No buyer. You couldn't wear them for years."

"So they'll be an investment."

"I can do this. Eight-fifty for the stones and one thousand for the gold. Those will have to come right apart."

*Hombre,* what bullshit! It was insulting, not the price itself, but attempting to hoodwink an intelligent person, one who could repeat a sequence of fourteen digits, could write out all his telephone numbers since childhood—a man who could, in a squinting instant, convert any odds to decimal form while the other jerks in the grandstand were still getting out their little Japanese calculators. Greenberg shook his head. Vicente shrugged. "Or else keep them yourself. Give them to your woman, maybe." Greenberg smiled at that, as one man of the world to another, which he intended as a compliment, for he was a man who three summers before had flown the Atlantic and gambled for fourteen days and thirteen nights in the casinos of Europe.

He got out of bed and, in bathrobe and slippers, went to the kitchen to join his wife and daughter. As he kissed them good morning he prayed that whatever might be coming would strike only him. Nevertheless a picture entered his head: himself sitting beside a hospital bed festooned with tubes. The idea hurt, and he felt guilty for enjoying the pain even briefly. This had become a habit that he wished he could break. If you let yourself take pleasure in such daydreams, the way you did in the faked suffering of actors, he felt that you were inviting grief and deserved it.

The radio was giving the weather—warm and sunny. His wife and daughter had finished breakfast and were clearing the table. They held their laden hands out from their bodies as they returned his kisses with coffeed lips. "We agreed you'd take us to the beach," his daughter said. "It's rully beautiful."

"I'll be showing properties all morning and afternoon," said Greenberg. "I'd like to, though." In apology he stroked her silky hair, her mother's mix of brown and blonde, salad-scented with the same shampoo. Claire held a telephone the same way Marilyn did, blew her nose the same, swam with the same swinging arc of arm and shoulder. Someday she'd turn out just as smart; you could see it starting almost by accident. Though Greenberg loved it, he wondered whether a son would have been like him. Women's nature seemed never his own. By contrast, he could feel an unflattering rapport with men who were total schmucks.

"Listen to this," Marilyn said. They were repeating the lead story: another report from some institute, Greenberg missed hearing which, warning that major earthquakes were likely soon. These predictions came in waves and had been frequent the last few months. He wondered whether an earthquake could be it, the intuition that was riding him today. If he asked, would he find that everyone in California had awakened this morning in nameless dread?

An ad for a fortified breakfast beverage followed the news, and Claire switched off the radio. "What's a temblor," she asked.

Marilyn gripped the edge of the drainboard and shook it gently. The dishes chattered. "It's this."

"I thought it was this." Claire clasped her hands above her head like a prizefight winner, rapidly shimmying her hips. It was things like that which worried Greenberg—he was sure she had no idea how suggestive it was—but with a tremendous effort he kept himself silent, sinking into a chair at the breakfast table and slumping forward with his face hidden in his folded arms.

"Ask Daddy," said his wife. "Barry, what's the difference between a temblor and a tremor?"

She was certain he would know, it was just the sort of

shadowy distinction he was good at, and her faith, as usual, buoyed him. Marilyn always granted him his due. What she loved about the stock market, she liked to tell people at poolside parties, at barbecues and bridge games, was that in the short run it was a voting machine, but in the long run it was a weighing machine—a description that suited Marilyn herself, Greenberg thought. She knew his assets, knew his liabilities, and was holding on for the long term.

It was, quoted Claire, sounding amused and surprised— as though a poem read at school had somehow created the fact—a marriage of true minds. Greenberg had met Marilyn in college, where bridge players gathered in a corner of the cafeteria. For him, a girl's appeal was $\left(\dfrac{IQ}{P}\right)\left(\dfrac{B}{V}\right)$, where P was pretension, B beauty, and V vanity, but he hadn't known her long before the calculation got out of hand.

Since then, had anything really changed? Evenings when they didn't play bridge they often played a nameless board game of Greenberg's invention. It began like chess but was won by compiling points rather than checkmate, and you could, for a price in pieces or points or board position (your opponent got to choose which), exchange the powers of your various pieces; you could also, once per game, alter the shape of the board, for a price that grew with the degree of change. Though Marilyn said Greenberg played more brilliantly, more creatively, she almost always won. Nights when he went to the races, she played racquetball and had a massage. A good life, Greenberg felt; what else could he want?

"*Daddy*," said Claire.

"Pardon?"

"Mother asked you a question."

"I'm sorry." He had thought he'd already answered. He raised his head from his arms. "I believe a tremor can be anything, like the palsy." Greenberg extended a rigid hand, which quivered more than he had expected. "Temblor is specific to earthquakes."

"Barry, can you have lunch with me?" Marilyn had her pocketbook. She would drop Claire at the bus stop. "Where will you be around noon?"

"All over," he said, though he knew he had said that too many times. "If I can meet you I'll call."

"Great. I'll leave lunch free."

"No, you'd better not."

When they were gone he felt a little safer. The mornings were always bad. He'd been staying in bed late and would have avoided his family entirely if he could. Each time he got through one of these breakfasts he felt grateful and surprised. Greenberg opened the morning paper, where Marilyn, or maybe Claire, had circled an article: about a man who for many years had secretly led a double life.

There had been uncomfortable looks, looks and

silences, but this circled article was the clearest sign yet that they were on to him.

Greenberg had been halfway shouldered out by his agency eight months ago. He still had stacks of business cards, and the switchboard operator would still jot down messages for him. But first they had told him he could no longer draw salary against commission, and then they had said that, given his productivity (stable, but it should have increased), they couldn't justify his desk space. He could, if he liked, share a single desk with a swarm of other losers.

His what? Physical person? No, it had nothing to do with his appearance. Everyone liked him, the office manager said. It was simply that they were too successful, expanding too rapidly, and the office, he could see for himself, was crowded with new and younger people, articulate and sexy, whose names he was not even told.

"Look, I've got something to deal with, my weight," Greenberg said, exhausted by hypocrisy, contemptuous of evasion. "Come back when I've dealt with it, right? Don't call us, we'll call you."

The office manager was embarrassed.

"Nobody trusts a fat man," said Greenberg. "Admit it, you phony."

That life was finished, he was afraid. But, maybe because it was ending in such a protracted way, he had never quite told Marilyn, or anyone else. His neighbor Katz, to whom Greenberg now waved as he made his way out to the car, loved to discuss real estate, forcing Greenberg to invent details of what he'd been showing and selling. This worried him; Katz was a lawyer and had recently been appointed some sort of prosecutor.

Greenberg stood in his driveway, wiping the condensation from his windshield. Katz was doing the same. "Late start, Barry," Katz called.

"I never stop," Greenberg called back. "I run all day. You sit on your fat tush."

"Listen, the way you're hauling it in. If I had——"

"Listen, if *I* had *your*——"

"If I had *half* your money——"

"Your money——"

They laughed. Greenberg was sweating. He waited until Katz had pulled away, with the confident acceleration of a man who cannot be given a ticket, before backing his Fairlane cautiously out into the street. When he stopped to buy gas he picked up a box of doughnuts. In a few minutes he had reached the freeway, where he swung up the ramp heading south.

It was showing homes that had given him the idea. Not that he hadn't daydreamed about it before—everyone must, he guessed, everyone with any brains or enterprise—in fact everyone. But it was showing wealthy homes, with the owners usually not even there, it was seeing how open everything lay, that had demonstrated the opportunity. Places he showed, in fact anything for sale, he never touched, because they'd look for an agent. He tried to be extremely careful. Greenberg had been furious when his own home was robbed, could have strangled the thief if he'd found him, and the memory of his rage stayed with him as a warning.

Any home where he saw a dog, an alarm box, protective iron grillwork, he didn't even consider. He would never enter a window, or try to force a door that had more than one lock. An artist at this or an athlete he wasn't—only careful. He would not carry tools. He never cruised a neighborhood more than once, enough to note certain houses with their owners' names on proud little signs. These he would find in the telephone book and call once a week, always at the same hour. If he got no answer to three or four calls, he went in.

He never attempted the largest, most elegant places, set at the end of winding drives. His father had always told him—and Greenberg believed it—his father had always said, with bitter admiration, that the big boys who really had it really knew how to hang on to it, too. It was guys like that, Marilyn's clients, the big shareholders who owned it all, the government, the trucks and the billboards, they were the ones who were somehow safe. Greenberg's only comfort was that they were mortal, and even that was changing—in their expensive private hospitals the heart-lung machines pumped away forever.

Driving south, going through the doughnuts, he gradually relaxed enough to enjoy the day. He pretended that he had agreed to the beach. He and Marilyn and Claire lay stretched in the sun, the tide rolling at their feet. With relief, like someone awakening from frightening dreams, he realized that he was thin. Soon he had passed the last of the billboards advertising Mexican automobile insurance—AAA, Seguridad, Sanborn's—and then he was easing up to a dock at the San Ysidro border station.

There was silence, except for the tapping and rattling of work in progress on Greenberg's car. He had better take the offer for the bracelets, he knew. But he could almost hear Vicente's whoop after Greenberg had left, how he might vaunt to the tiny mechanic, bursts and streamers of Spanish breaking into derisive falsetto. That sound would fill the car on Greenberg's homeward drive. He'd be all over the road, punching seat cushions. Not just because Vicente was getting rich, would buy himself a block of gray apartments and a pastel villa on the Pacific—there was a principle of justice involved. Let yourself be screwed once and history showed what would follow. "Do a little better than that," he said.

Vicente shrugged. He never bargained. And Greenberg found himself rewrapping the bracelets in tissues, then in flannel. He felt shaky but couldn't stop. Vicente was counting out hundreds and fifties onto the grimy desk top. When he got to the total on his pad he looked up. "Last time. I'll take those off your hands." Greenberg shook his head—fat chance, you slob! Then, with frightening suddenness, Vicente had squeezed Greenberg's hand (caught limp in its surprise) and was gone.

Greenberg tucked the wrapped bracelets back inside the hubcap of his spare. He had no idea what he would do with them. The little man came crawling out of the pit. "You need new shocks," he said, and Greenberg, seeing the thinness of his arms and neck, had the urge to take him out to lunch. The mechanic wrote up a careful statement for the muffler: parts and labor. Greenberg paid him. The sagging garage door was swung open, and, with his sixth new muffler of the year, he pulled out into the blinding brightness of the street. Approaching the border, he remembered to search the glove compartment for his last muffler bill and stuff it under his seat.

He had never before crossed into the U.S. carrying anything stolen, and his saliva seemed salty as he pulled up to American customs. At the last moment he grabbed Vicente's cellophane bag from his lap, though it still held a few broken corn chips in its bottom corners, and shoved it under his seat.

"Please state your citizenship," the official told him. He was very young, with elaborate waves of red hair and a mottled, scaly complexion that made Greenberg wonder whether he'd been in a fire.

"American," said Greenberg.

"Did you buy anything?"

"No. I had my car serviced. I've got the slip."

He guessed that the boy would now drop to push-up position and peer under the car. This had happened several times; one leather-faced chief inspector had pulled Greenberg out of line and tapped the new muffler with a little rubber mallet. But the boy scarcely glanced at Greenberg's bill before handing it back. "Drive carefully," he said. "We just heard there's been an earthquake."

"I never even knew it," Greenberg said in wonder. His first sensation was release—maybe this was all it was, the thing he'd been feeling would happen today. "Where was the epicenter?"

Then he thought of Marilyn at work in her skyscraper, Claire at school, and socked his chest in terror. The boy was watching him closely. "It's nothing to worry about," he said. "The traffic hasn't changed at all."

Greenberg smashed his chest twice more, now in remorse for his stubbornness with Vicente: he would have to keep within the speed limit, considering what was in his trunk. "Heart?" asked the boy.

"No, I'm fine."

"You don't look good. Better pull off into that parking area." He pointed. "If you're sick I can call an ambulance."

Yes! That was exactly, stunningly, what Greenberg wanted, to be brought to a coronary care unit, laid in a bed, each stroke of his heart televised, recorded, understood. "Don't worry," he said. "This is the way I look." He took off, careful to keep his acceleration moderate.

Heading north, past billboard ads for discount gas and economy motels and airline flights to Las Vegas, he could spot no certain signs of an earthquake, but what would they be? A greenhouse had some broken panes; a Qantas billboard (FLY DOWN UNDER) was sagging. He cried a little. His relief at not finding devastation was weirdly mixed with fresh dread.

When he pulled into his street he saw that Katz's Mazda was back in its driveway. Greenberg shut his car door quietly. Inside, he hurriedly checked the doors and windows, his habit ever since his wedding silver was stolen, and then, back in the kitchen, telephoned Marilyn.

When he heard her voice he felt that there was hope. "Are you okay?" he asked. "I heard—"

"I'm all right," she said, but her exaggerated calm told him that she had been badly frightened. "It seemed worse than it was because this building's designed to sway. I had coffee on my desk and it went all over my clothes."

"Did you call Claire's school?"

"She's fine. They hardly felt it there. There might be stronger shocks coming, the radio said."

"Come home," said Greenberg. "We'll get into bed."

"I would love to. But you told me I should make a lunch appointment."

"That's okay."

"There's cold chicken."

"It was you I wanted," he said, raising his elbows so she could put her arms around his body.

"You have me, Barry."

"That's okay. I was showing some homes in Chula Vista all morning. I have to run up north this afternoon."

"Barry," she said, and Greenberg knew from the tenderness in her voice that something bad was coming. "I called your office."

"What for?"

"What do you mean, what for? To make sure you were okay. They said you weren't with them anymore."

Marilyn worked at one of eight desks in a room where stock transactions flashed ceaselessly across the wall. Greenberg could picture her now, gaze forward—New York would be closed, but not yet the Pacific Exchange—unconsciously monitoring the market. "There's a new switchboard girl," he said.

"It was Caroline. She remembered you. She remembered *me*."

"Anyhow, she's wrong. I'm a part of that office. I've been working out of the Chula Vista branch, the last few weeks."

"Barry," Marilyn said. "Don't cry, baby. We'll sit down—"

"Sure."

"Okay?"

"Sure," he said. "We'll go out for dinner, huh? I made some money today."

Somehow or other he would handle this, that was all Greenberg knew. Intuitive! That was his personal style, what Marilyn claimed she envied in him. By tomorrow this would all be settled. Tomorrow was coming, swinging like a scythe from the International Date Line at what velocity?

The earth's circumference over twenty-four, a thousand thirty-something miles per hour. Then this pain would be gone. Time was merciful, if a person knew how to use it.

As he drove, the sea off to his left flickering in the afternoon light, he thought of sitting down with his wife, later with his daughter—maybe at sunset, on a cliff above a beach at Point Loma—and telling them the truth. He could hear the waves below, could feel soft hands begin to comfort his shoulders and the back of his neck. Just past the city limits he left the freeway and headed inland, up into the hills. If Marilyn and Claire really loved him, he wondered angrily, why hadn't they seen what was going on?

White brick, mission tile roof. The house stood beyond a broad green lawn, hidden from its neighbors by towering hedges of oleander. Greenberg would have priced it in the one nineties. He parked around the corner and approached on foot. The driveway was empty, the Venetian blinds uniformly horizontal. There was no sound of life. He rang the two-chime doorbell, waited, rang it again, then walked around to the back, tugging on dish-washing gloves of elastic rubber.

With two kicks he smashed the back door loose from its frame. It swung inward, its lock protruding pathetically. Always, when this moment came, Greenberg felt himself start to float, as though he were breathing nitrous. He stepped inside and quickly found the master bedroom suite, the dressing room off the custom-tiled bath, the jewel box left right out on the vanity, and thrust into his pockets everything that gleamed. Back in the bedroom he tossed clothing in a blizzard from dresser drawers—nothing—and then stepped into the man's paneled study, whose closet made it a natural guest room. In a desk drawer he found a monogrammed pocket watch. Enough; his body knew it was time to go, as surely as, when he dived into the Pacific, it knew when to surface. On his way out he passed through the kitchen, where someone had left taped to the refrigerator a red-lettered reminder: VOTE TODAY.

Then he was back in his car, starting the engine. But he found himself sitting there while the Fairlane idled. Something, at first incomprehensible, was drawing him back to the house. He grew aware of a bulge against his thigh— the monogrammed watch. The horrifying thought of returning it now entered his head, and he drove past the front of the house and flung the watch desperately onto the lawn. Pulling off his rubber gloves, he continued on toward the freeway. The watch's ghost rode with him, a closeup of it lying in the thick grass.

He had almost reached the freeway when he made a U-turn and headed back up into the hills, steering with one hand, the other knotted in his hair. This was it, the police would be there by now. "Fool," he said. From him his whole life had been stolen, and now it wept for ransom. "Idiot, ass!" He drove faster, and when he reached the house it looked as abandoned as before. On hands and knees he searched the lawn, furious at his stupidly clawing fingers. Then they fell upon the watch. Almost running, he replaced it in its drawer in the study, and hurried back out through the hardwood-cabinet-lined kitchen.

In the spacious laundry room, just off the kitchen, he now noticed an enormous wicker basket, and, resting on its top edge, the great gray head of what appeared to be a dog. Greenberg froze, wondering if he was going crazy. The head looked artificial, hallucinatory—could a dog have been sleeping there all this time? "Hello, sweetheart," he said, smiling, afraid that the dog would smell his sweat. "Hello, angel." He began to walk very slowly toward the rear of the house, wondering if he would be able to shut the shattered back door behind him.

The gray dog stood and stretched, then stepped out of its basket, one stiff leg at a time. It advanced slowly as Greenberg retreated. It was gigantic, the kind he thought was called a staghound, obviously old and weak. "Go back to sleep, angel," Greenberg said. If necessary he thought he could outrun it.

But the dog was coming on faster now, and caught him at the door. He was afraid to turn his back on it. It wasn't growling, just lolling out its tremendous tongue, so he reached forward to make friends. It would be content, he guessed, if he let it sniff him and lick his hand. He peeled off a glove.

The dog nuzzled his fingers, poked its hot nostrils into the center of his palm, where he had always found it erotic to be touched, then sank its teeth into his palm's fleshy outer edge.

It was a feeble bite, and the dog's jaws were so weak that he was able to slap them apart with his free hand. The old dog whined piteously, as though Greenberg were the attacker, and backed away with difficulty. Halfway across the room its legs gave out. It collapsed on the floor in a helpless heap, watching him with blank wet eyes.

"Damn you," said Greenberg. He could tell that the wound wasn't serious, but it hurt and was bleeding vigorously, each toothmark welling red. He held it away from him and hurried, dripping, back to the car. On the dashboard were tissues, which he wadded around his hand. He stuffed the rubber gloves under his seat, taking deep breaths to calm himself. Then he drove away slowly, guiding the steering wheel with his left knee.

Though he doubted that he could bleed to death, he thought he might faint if the bleeding didn't stop; he had to get home immediately and apply pressure. Nevertheless, up on the freeway he made himself hold it at fifty-five. By the year 2000, freeways would be automated, Marilyn had told him. The companies she bought and sold were taking care of that. You would enter, get in your lane, and elements in the roadbed would drive your car; the thought left Greenberg amazed and uneasy. He wrapped more tissues around his wound. He would be able to explain this. Showing homes, anybody could be bitten.

As he approached his exit, traffic grew thick in the

right-hand lane, and partway down the ramp he was brought to a full stop. In a moment he was trapped by cars piling up behind him. His hand was hurting less now, but the soaked tissues were starting to fall apart, and the box was empty. He shoved it under his seat. Greenberg wondered whether he should abandon the car, get out and walk, find a phone and call Marilyn.

The line crawled forward and stopped, stopped and crawled in spasms, and soon he could see what was causing the delay. A hundred yards beyond the bottom of the exit ramp, police cruisers were pulled up on both sides of the road. His first thought was that there must be earthquake damage ahead—he pictured streets littered with glass and brick, the parted lips of fissures. Then he guessed that the police were only checking licenses and registrations, looking for stolen cars.

He would keep his injured hand out of sight. There would be no way for them to guess that his pockets were filled with jewelry, that two jeweled bracelets lay in the hubcap of his spare. But even as he crept forward in line, even as he tugged his license from his wallet and his registration from the glove compartment, the sense that disaster was coming right now gushed up in him. It was as though some artery, swelling since morning, had finally blown out its wall.

Above him, thundering trucks rumbled by on the freeway, which curved off into the distance and out of sight. Weeping, Greenberg leaned on his horn. But after a minute he could scarcely hear it. Instead he seemed to feel it; the muted sound might have been in his bones, like the reverberations of a dentist's drill. Though he was still well back in line, one policeman was walking up the ramp toward him, and he saw several others watching. And it really was as though Greenberg were having some form of dentistry. Moment by moment he could feel his dread leaving him, the knowledge of doom that had oppressed him all day—could feel it drawn out of him like some great, many-rooted tooth pulled from every part of his body—until at last, when the uniformed figure dimmed his window, everything he had felt was gone, leaving within him an absence that he probed with awe.

# Sailing Home

ON A MAP, OR BETTER A GLOBE, I COULD show you where I met her.

We were the first night out on the Queen Elizabeth 2, and they'd said over the loudspeakers we were a hundred miles west of Ireland. I wasn't thinking about girls, I'm not the kind that does. This crossing I had a project—starting a sort of history, family history, a history of my family. I may be the last of us.

So I went to the writing room, and they have this very thin airmail paper with Cunard on it and a profile of the ship, and I thought about my grandfather—he came the same direction by sea. Broke: he touched his pockets proudly every time he told me that. I held a pen with both hands and remembered his fingers, fat like they'd been blown up with water, touching and tapping his pockets.

You know his name. He started Samuel Levy Furs, Fifth Avenue.

So from the writing room I went to the Club Lido— that's the First Class nightclub, you see it in the Cunard brochure—and they had a singer on, her big glossy photo

on a tripod by the door, you know those pictures—all long
dark hair and big dark eyes—The Sensational Madeline
Lee, it said underneath. Inside was Madeline. She sat on a
high stool, legs crossed and one heel hooked over a rung,
and a red curtain hanging in folds behind her and her piano
player, and I've seen many attractive singers, but this one
was different, or something was. I knew in five seconds that
something was different.

She had a low voice for a woman, with a rawness in it.
She never gestured, just moved her head from side to side,
looking at everyone, and she did it all with her eyes and her
voice. A girl that young and slim. There wasn't a sound in
the room while she sang—you could just see the cigarette
smoke curling up from the tables, and tiny suns reflecting
off a percussion set—and under the floor you could feel
the ship's big screws vibrate through the water, spinning at
the ends of their shafts.

I fell, what, in love with her that night?
I hardly believe that love exists at all, except in a few
people—like genius. I'm no genius—I admit that. I don't
know anyone who's a genius, and I don't think I know
anyone who really loves anyone else.
I'll say this: I fell under her spell.
My guess was she was lovers with her piano player, a
really athletic-looking young guy—they were flashing
each other smiles all evening. She was probably having a
last drink with him in their cabin and getting into bed with

him right now. So don't think I ever had one dream, not one small hope, I'd get anywhere with her. I just felt like I'd die if I didn't. And of course I knew I wouldn't die either—I'd just end up a little different in some bad way.

I lay awake, feeling the rolling of the ship, all night. At about four I got up and climbed to the boat deck, and stood looking down at the water boiling along, black with sometimes the white crest of a chesty wave. My father would have called her a *bummerkeh* and never looked at her again—this was a man who lived only for business—and I said I've never known a genius, but if anyone came close it was my father. He'd have been amazed to see this happening to me.

During the night I could feel the ship rolling much worse, and the next morning people were staggering. I took it slow—if I turned an ankle, with my weight, that'd be it—my ankles are weak anyway, I can't dance and so forth. Breakfast didn't interest me this morning. Aft, one deck is reserved for First Class, and I went there and lay in a deck chair.

The way we were rolling I knew better than to try and read. I folded my hands on my stomach and shut my eyes and thought about that pretty young singer, and it hit me harder than ever. Everything that was good in my life seemed to turn to, I don't know, just photos of things that were good—they were no use to me anymore. I lay there in the sun with my eyes closed, and maybe slept, until the deck steward came around, just like it states in the brochure, to ask if I wanted consommé. I shook my head without opening my eyes. So he asked the person in the next chair—I didn't even know there was anyone there. The voice that answered him, I recognized it right away, was her: Madeline.

She said yes to the consommé, and I admit I let it get to me, how nice I could hear her being to the steward. A while longer and I opened my eyes and stretched. Madeline had her deck chair propped up, she was sipping consommé and reading a paperback. I could see the cover. One thing I could tell her was there were better books than that—I buy the Editors' Choice, not the Best Sellers.

"Excuse me," I said. She turned her whole head, and I felt like her eyes would knock me over the side of the ship, she was so close and so pretty. And she had that power, like she was still on stage. "I didn't have any. Normally it's too salty for me. How is it?"

"I know you," she said. "You were at the show last night. You were the one at the table in front by yourself." She sounded interested, and I knew I looked pretty good. I have my grandfather's jaw and shoulders, and my mother's eyes, and I learned from my father that you don't dress cheap.

"You were great," I said.

"Thank you," she said, and smiled, and that was that—no asking how did I like this number or how she actually had a cold—she was ready to drop it right there. "Are you on business or pleasure? But no one takes the QE2 on business, do they."

"I've been sight-seeing," I explained. "France and mostly Switzerland. I got on at Cherbourg."

A woman likes it, my mother told me, if a man has money—it makes her feel protected. Madeline was nodding, as though she hadn't been to those countries and thought I wouldn't like her if I knew. "Did you ski?" She was trying to sound sophisticated but missing by a mile, and I knew I'd remember the way she asked that all my life.

"I can't ski," I told her. "I have some kind of weakness in my ankles. Of all stupid places."

She didn't smile. Instead she looked concerned, so that I felt like leaning over and kissing her. "Can't you exercise them?"

"My orthopedist says no."

And now she did smile. "I never learned to ski either," she said. "What do you do for a living?"

When the honest truth is you don't do one useful thing in the world, you get very smooth at answering that question. "We're in the fur business," I said. Next she was going to ask me what I did in the fur business, and I'd say I was in a supervisory capacity.

But what she said was, "I'm a child of the garment industry too. My father's a tailor."

A child too—like we were the same generation. "I'm Martin Levy," I said, and would have reached across to shake her hand, except she still had her paperback in one hand, closed around a finger that was keeping her place, and in the other hand her cup of consommé. I would have done it anyway, and made her put the book down, just to show I was comfortable with beauty—you want beauty, you should see what walks into our shop all day—but she had something else that paralyzed me.

"Madeline Lee," she said. "Look at that, we have the same initials." And her face curled as though she'd discovered we were old classmates, something intimate, something from the far past. "It's my professional name. I'm really Lefkowitz." And she put down the book and reached across to shake *my* hand. Hers was small and strong and—I guess from the warm cup of soup—warm.

Now, I'd thought she might be Jewish. People named Levy always wonder about people named Lee. And her knocking me over, I mean emotionally, had nothing to do with that. But if there could be anything that would tie me up tighter, that was it. My mother is still alive, not healthy but alive, and if I ever did get married I would rather for her sake, I mean my mother's, that the girl was Jewish. "A pleasure," I said. I held her hand a minute to show her the way I felt. That's when I noticed the wedding ring on her other one.

It didn't bother me one bit. I mean there were already so many other reasons why she'd never want me, what did it matter? I was actually glad, because it took the pressure off. But it also gave me one more thing to think about, even though I knew I was just lowering myself in deeper.

"I see you're married," I said, letting go of her hand. "Is your husband the piano player?"

She shook her head quickly. "Thank God no. He only likes men, in fact."

"Is your husband a singer also?"

"He's a graduate student at Columbia. In American Studies. He's doing his thesis on Bellow. Do you like Bellow?"

Now, I know Bellow. Not Bellow, I mean—his literary works. They used to be New and Recommended, before Editors' Choice even existed. But I knew better than to start in with Madeline. She'd begin telling me about her husband's thesis and I wouldn't understand it. "I haven't read enough of him," I said.

"I'll lend you," she said. "I carry some with me. Not this." She reached down and snapped a fingernail against her best-seller, like she was getting rid of something disgusting. "My accompanist's," she said. "Schlock."

How insulting it was, in a way—but she looked at me so full in the eyes, like she was talking about saving my soul, like she really *would* save it, if I'd let her—that I just felt myself get weaker. I won't try to describe it, you've either felt that way or you haven't, and if you haven't I pity you— I pity you either way. "What's he like," I said. "Your husband."

She stretched, pointing her toes. "We get along pretty well. Except we're really poor. This is the first really good-paying job I've had."

The ship was rolling more than ever, Madeline and I swaying so much that I was afraid it looked silly. "I'd better go in," she said. "I had to wear my second-best outfit last night because my first-best was ripped. I've got to sew it up."

"Don't they have someone who'll do that for you?"

"I wouldn't trust them. My father's a tailor, remember. I carry a sewing kit."

She stood, staggering a few steps as the deck shifted. I reached out an arm but she got her balance. "Martin, it was really nice talking to you." From the heart, that seemed. "Will I see you at the show tonight?" I said she would.

Madeline smiled. Then, with tiny careful steps, she walked away. The rolling of the deck made her cross it in a zigzag, like a little boat herself, tacking against the wind.

It seems it's always this way—you don't know what makes you feel the way you do. Most of that day, I lay on my bed and felt faint from the motion of the ship, and from not having had any breakfast or lunch. And that got confused with the way Madeline made me feel. I'm not saying I suffered—I think only a few people ever really suffer—but it was like nothing else that ever happened to me. Maybe it's the age I've reached, or somehow the fact we were on a ship—I never felt such, I don't know, despair. My apartment, my car, my paintings, my friends, the restaurants where they know me, everything I own, everything I ever did—I imagined God or someone saying I could have Madeline if I gave up all the rest, and I grabbed her.

Then I began thinking, lying there on my bed, about the steward who'd brought the consommé, how nice she'd been to him, and whether she'd been just the same to us both. To me she'd been really sweet, but that could have been just her nature. If the sun shines, that doesn't mean it loves you, or if a bird sings—you get the way I was thinking.

In late afternoon the rolling eased up, but I felt too impatient for dinner and just had a platter of sandwiches brought to my cabin. Then I spent a few dollars on the fruit machines in the casino, and drank some Glenfiddich at the casino bar.

When it got to be time for Madeline's show I was pretty far gone—I was looking on the wrong deck for the Club Lido. When I finally found it, all the front tables were filled. I sat in back, next to a tray filled with little triangles of club sandwich stuck through with fancy toothpicks. They show those in the brochure, except in the brochure the tray is silver.

I could see why her first-best dress was first-best. She'd been pretty last night, but tonight she was gorgeous. I knew I'd had too much to drink. But I couldn't believe that was why every note she sang hit me like a harpoon, or why she looked so—I don't know—magical, when she sang "Over the Rainbow" and the gels of the spotlight bled through all the colors, starting her in darkness and ending up in brilliant white. She saw me and smiled, and I waved.

But when she took her first break and I wanted to buy her a drink some big fat bald guy—I carry a lot of weight, but I'd never let myself get like this guy—got there first, and moved her and her piano player over to the bar. Maybe he was a real funnyman, but he had her in stitches, all through the set the next group was doing, so she half fell over, catching herself on his arm, and he put his other arm around her shoulders for a second. Her piano player wasn't laughing, and I thought I saw him give me a look, kind of a well-what-do-you-expect look. She must have told him something about me, just the way she told me about him, and I thought that was lousy of her.

Then, at the end of Madeline's second set, she did something that I think I'll think about every day for the rest of my life. "Now I'd like to sing one of my very favorite tunes," she said, and climbed down from her tall stool. "But I need a gentleman to assist me."

She looked out over the crowd. "Anyone here named Marmaduke?"

Chuckles.

"All right, I'll take an Ebenezer."

"Me Charlie," some drunk called.

She laughed like it was a really clever joke. "How about Martin," she called, not looking at me. "Any Martins?"

I was on my feet in a second and scrambling forward between the tables like some sort of ape, knocking against people, tilting their drinks—I don't know, I didn't look back. All I saw was what was happening ahead of me. The fat bald guy was getting up from his front table, walking forward onto the hardwood. He reached her just ahead of me.

"Martin Levy," I practically shouted.

He looked back over his shoulder. "Sorry, Martin. I'm Martin Luther."

Everyone howled. They were on his side. But I looked past him at Madeline and I saw, I swear to God I did, the pain on her face—she hadn't planned this, she didn't want this to be happening to me. Any other time I would have just sat down, but now never. "Identification!" I yelled, and whipped out my wallet. They all laughed while I hunted for my driver's license, but I finally found it and pressed it into Madeline's hand.

She read it out loud and clear. "Levy, Martin Isaac." There were cheers. A few boos.

The fat guy had out a credit card, and was holding it toward her, but half covered up. She tried to get it out of his hand, the whole meaty paw up to her face, while he hung on, grinning, and the crowd was yelling. Finally she got it loose. "Arthur Greenfield," she called. There were boos, cheers, applause, whistles. "Siddown, Art," someone yelled, and then two women he'd been sitting with came and pulled him off the floor.

Madeline gave the sign to her piano player, who was looking disgusted, and I recognized the intro, but it wasn't until she raised her arms to me and sang "I . . . could . . . have . . . da-a-anced all night" that I understood what she was offering.

And here I was with weak ankles. Like I told you, I don't dance—it's too risky for me.

But I did. What else could I do, after what she'd done, and if this didn't show she felt something, then what did? I was careful, and she let me go after a few turns. Back in my chair, I crossed first one leg and then the other, feeling my ankles. My head was spinning as I watched her finish the song. Let's not talk about love. But I'll tell you this, and nothing that happened later will make me deny it—I felt joy. I did. Joy.

And it was like when I yelled "Identification!" a new life started for me, because the rest of that evening went like magic. After she closed her last set I got her to the casino bar, and we talked there, and I held her hand, and it was all just as natural as it could be. She said how nervous she'd been about the Martin thing and thanked me for demanding identification, she said what presence of mind I had. I remembered that the Captain's cocktail party for First Class passengers was tomorrow and suggested we go together—she said yes, let's. It came out that my family was Samuel Levy Furs, Fifth Avenue. Madeline said she'd been by and admired our pieces, and I said we didn't do endangered species, and she said she didn't have any furs at all, her husband would hit the roof if she even bought fox or rabbit at the Salvation Army, he was so left-wing, he thought it was a sign of God knows what, and I said, I don't know what, maybe I just looked understanding, and it came out what a difficult marriage she had, and we had more to drink, and I told her about myself, how I'd never been married and so forth. So the bar closed. So I walked her to the elevators.

And I knew, if I ever knew anything in my life, that if I asked her to come to my cabin, she'd come—she wanted to come with me—I knew it, I could feel it. But my mouth was like it was sewed together. And the elevator arrived, and I punched my deck button, and, God help me, I couldn't help looking at her, and then she had to tell me her deck, and it was a different deck, and that was that.

I lay in bed, and I was never so furious at myself in my life.

But only at first.

Then I realized I'd been pretty lucky. Because it was true—she was nice to everyone, the consommé steward and the fat bald guy just as much as me. And yes, we'd become close at the bar, and that had been genuine, but I guessed she could have gotten that close with almost anyone. It was just the way she was.

And if I slept with her, that wouldn't mean a thing to her—why should it, when any man on the ship would have done it? But to me, the way I felt about her, it would have meant so much that just the thought of it frightened me—not making love itself, but what my feelings would be like afterward.

I realized that it would be better just meeting her at the Captain's cocktail party. I'd keep coming to her shows. In New York we could meet for dinner. Maybe she'd accept a gift of furs—if her husband couldn't see them I'd keep them for her, she could wear them just when she was with me. I kept thinking of her calling for Martins, and myself demanding "Identification!", and I was never so proud and happy in my life.

The next day it was past noon when I woke up, and my head was killing me. But that wasn't all. I suspected it while I lay in bed another hour, trying to fall back asleep. And I found out for certain when I tried to get up for my Bufferin and mouthwash. My ankles were aching, both of them.

It wasn't so bad. I couldn't even blame it definitely on the dancing—sometimes they just ache a little. But I held it against Madeline anyway, my ankles and head both. I guessed she was feeling not so good herself, and maybe not so good about me, and now I was really grateful for whatever had kept us from making love.

I dozed off and on all afternoon, and by five o'clock felt mostly better. Then I spent too long in the bath and had to shave quickly. I combed my hair and patted on my cologne and got into my underwear. I flicked my shoes with a towel.

Then I got into my tux. It was just seven on the dot when I tugged my bow tie straight and saw in the wall mirror that my fly was visible. The zipper wasn't broken— the fabric was just pulled to the sides so you could see the gleam of the metal teeth.

I pushed the button for the stewardess, then the button for the steward—all it would take was setting the hooks so the waist was right. Then I stood there minute after minute, getting panicky, because Madeline was waiting for me. So finally I thought of Madeline herself, Madeline and her sewing kit. I dialed her room but of course she wasn't there, she'd already be at the bar.

So I dialed the bar—don't ask me how I got the nerve. I asked for Miss Madeline Lee. I heard them calling her name.

"Hello?"

"Madeline?"

"Martin?"

"Madeline," I said, "I've had an accident, can you come to my room?"

"Are you okay?"

"Can you do that for a minute? And sew something for me?" I got it out one word at a time, but I was sweating, and I knew, don't ask me how, I knew already that she wouldn't. There was too much going on in the background, or it was the excitement in her voice. It was nothing against me. She just wasn't going to come.

"What is it," she asked. "Not your—not the seat of your—"

"No, nothing that funny."

"No, it's not funny at all," she said, and you could tell she was trying to keep her voice serious. She was trying to be nice about this. "Martin, I'm with some people, and the party's really begun—I just saw the Captain, I think it was him—can you understand? We'll meet after my show—is that okay?"

"I don't know. Look—"

"Look, I—"

"If you don't—"

"No, I will, if you really, really, want me to. Only why don't you just change?"

"Sure," I said. "That's what I'll do."

"If you want me to come I will, only—"

I hung up and I was just boiling. I thought I'd go and be very cold to her. But when I got my tux off, and stood there looking at myself in my underwear—they have these huge mirrors, to make the cabin seem bigger—I knew I couldn't go. I look my best in a tux. I couldn't go out dressed wrong, not feeling the way I was. I'd be the only guy there who wasn't formal.

Anyway, I had something else to do. I sat down, and it never felt so good to take the weight off my ankles. I had my family history to think about. I thought of my father, the expression on his face if he could know what I was feeling, and my grandfather, smiling and touching his pockets. I got out my pen, and some of that thin Cunard stationery, and began to write.

So a minute later the phone rang. I didn't answer it. I'm innocent, I admit it, I don't know what the hell to do, maybe I'm a failure—that's all, no shame in that—but one thing I do know, I know when I've blown it. I know when I'm finished. I don't chase what can't be mine—I've always prided myself on that.

And my being a failure—that's not true either, exactly. I don't think anyone in the world is really a failure. I've got plenty going for me—I won't talk about material things, but I have some damn good friends. When we docked, one of them was there to meet me, the guy who manages our shop.

Even so, it's been months, but I'm still thinking about Madeline. And I feel terrifically sorry for her, sorry for what she'll learn about life—lots of things I never got the chance to tell her or warn her about.

One thing especially, a type she needs to watch out for: people like her. I wish I could teach her that. Sometimes I stand in the front of our shop, where the mannequins look out at Fifth Avenue. I stand on a Persian carpet where we keep our display of pelts. People are always stopping, and some day I know I'll see Madeline up against the glass.

Then I'll go out and warn her right there on the sidewalk: some people, they seem terrific, you think they really like you, and it turns out that's only the way they are. It isn't you at all—it's them, it's all them, it's always them, it's only them. People like her, I will explain—"People like you," I'll say, "don't mean to be cruel, they just don't mean to be anything," I'll warn her, "any more than the Statue of Liberty is really glad to see you," I'll say, "or the doorman who takes your bags from the cab actually cares if you live or die."

# Articles on the Heart

IS HIGH SCHOOL HAD SUSPENDED
him for setting fires, and then his parents had
started in. So Duane had left New Rochelle and
hitchhiked to Sandra's and Otis's house in Mamaroneck.
For as long as he could remember, he had been secretly in
love with his older cousin, though it was a secret he
guessed and hoped she knew. He could never forget one
hug Sandra had given him when he was in junior high
school, stabbing her breasts into the top of his stomach as
though she had no idea how amazing that felt.

She had really gained weight since then, and Duane saw
the minute he walked in that she had no bra on underneath
her muumuu. He wasn't even sure if they made a bra that
would hold those mammoth beauties. If they did he would
like to see it, not that she would ever show it to him.

"Now I've got nothing," he told Otis, and, when he
heard his voice whine like a child's, momentarily felt like
smashing himself in the face. He knew he would never, not
when he was fifty, be an adult the way Otis was. It wasn't
things, it was how they were put together—Otis's shoul-

ders, tennis serve, Mercedes diesel, the thick black hairs that pierced the weave of his polo shirt.

Otis smiled. "You've got time," he said, in a tone that might have been either amused or irritated.

"Now I'll find out what real suffering means, is what my mother told me."

"They'll get over it," said Sandra. "You're staying with us awhile. Otis can get you a job on Wall Street. Would you be a delivery boy?"

"I'll look around," Otis said. He threw another log on the fire. Watching it sear and smoke, Duane felt, with the tremulous emotion that was what he hated most in himself: so this is my life. Up in flames.

When Sandra got out of bed, the coals of the fire still glowed in the darkened living room, and the bricks before the fireplace were warm to her bare feet. Otis was snoring. Behind Duane's closed door there was silence.

The moment she opened the refrigerator, caught sight of the food and felt the cold downdraft on her shins, she began to salivate. She took out mustard, butter, mayonnaise, Swiss cheese, Polish ham. She made two sandwiches and poured herself a glass of milk.

Sandra could diet all day, but at night felt so empty that she would visualize each shelf in the refrigerator, the gleaming white and silver, the bright packages and glittering foil wrappings. It was a clean and happy scene, and it made her feel, more than clothes or cars or the house ever did, how rich and lucky she was.

She felt like a beauty out of folklore, swallowed by a vast beast. The more her friends insisted that she carried it well, the less Sandra could share a room or lawn with slim girls in jeans, girls in narrow-waisted long dresses, tennis whites, bathing suits. At parties, she had seen men face away from her, toward girls with slim arms and clean chinlines, as involuntarily as her houseplants turned their leaves toward the window. She tried not to buy anything fattening, but as she walked the bright supermarket aisles the sight of the familiar packages, the aromas of the deli and bakery counters, overcame her. She daydreamed of an operation in which her fat would be sliced cleanly away.

Toward Otis she felt bitter. He never encouraged her, never criticized her. Leftovers he always left, even when she guessed he was starved. He seemed to want her to be fat, so he would have an excuse for affairs. Lately he was hardly making love to her at all, and Sandra tried not to develop an image of the slim girl she was sure he was sleeping with.

She finished her second sandwich and went back to the refrigerator. There was leftover casserole, still good. But Sandra ate only a small portion, because she planned to reheat some for Duane's lunch. Now she wished she hadn't urged him to stay. Her feelings about him, his height and slenderness, his blue eyes that got caught on her bust, were foolish—he was only, what, seventeen? She finished the maple walnut ice cream, and had a little black raspberry ice cream. Then, stuffed, she washed her dishes and turned out the kitchen light.

The living room's sliding glass doors looked out on nothing but woods. Dusted with snow, the motionless branches seemed turned to stone. Sometimes, on nights like this, Sandra could stare into the trees until she forgot who she was. A ghost of the cold touched her through the glass, and she wondered how quickly she would die out among the frozen trees. Her skin tautened into gooseflesh. She lay down on the carpet, her bathrobe parted, and her hand slid under her nightgown to cup her crotch.

There was no sound from Duane's room. Sandra stared at the ceiling, and saw there what would happen in the morning. Otis would leave while Duane was still asleep. She would take a shower. She would shave her legs and perfume herself. Then she would kneel beside Duane's bed, lean close, her breasts on the pillow beside him, and stroke him awake.

Otis had slept badly and opened his eyes several times to find Sandra gone. He wondered whether she had crawled into bed with Duane. But when he awoke for the last time, at six, she was heaped beside him.

He dressed quietly and had a glass of orange juice. Sandra had finished the ham and most of the Swiss, he saw. In the garbage, under a paper towel, he found a neatly folded ice cream carton.

No rush, he told himself, but his pedal foot was trained to hold sixty-five. Driving slowly made Otis feel nervous as an escapee. To see the landscape, of which he knew every bush and utility pole, sliding past so gradually reminded him of dreams in which his limbs waved slowly no matter how he struggled to run. Otis was tired and his eyes hurt. Lately he had been leaving the house earlier and earlier, whenever he woke up, sometimes before daylight.

He felt certain that this life was killing him. With a warm rush of love he pictured himself as he had been at sixteen, sophisticated and indestructible. In his album was a picture of himself at that age, bare-chested behind the wheel of a convertible jeweled with chrome. Now Otis was at an age when he knew the worst things began to happen, invisibly, in the arteries and organs. He tried to avoid refined sugars, and read every article he saw on cholesterol and the heart.

When he reached Manhattan he pulled into the basement garage of his lover's apartment building. For several months he had had no office. He had told Sandra he was looking for a new one, and that in the meantime he was working in boardrooms. But all he really needed was a telephone, and there was one on the table by Jeffrey's bed. Otis was incorporated as Growth Management Associates and was the manager of twenty-three portfolios, belonging mostly to friends of Sandra's father. He had once worked at them full-time, but they did as well—or, recently, as badly—if he ignored them. Once a day he phoned for quotes, and once a week he spent the afternoon calling his clients. Jeffrey would operate an electric typewriter in the background; he had never had the patience to learn the keyboard but had captured an authentic rhythm.

Otis let himself in. Jeffrey was still sleeping. He tiptoed

to the bedroom and undressed by habit. When he got into bed Jeffrey nestled against him sleepily and began to caress him.

But Otis was distracted, worried about the Geller account, which he had leveraged to meet the margin requirement on the Breitbart account. If he got caught juggling accounts he could go to jail. He hadn't been willing, hadn't felt able, to liquidate Breitbart's oils or aerospace, especially after he had given the man such assurances. It seemed safe, at least for a month or two, to transfer cash from Geller, who rarely asked questions. Jeffrey began to press hard against him. "I think I'll make some calls first," Otis said, but let Jeffrey ease him over and Vaseline him. Behind the bed was a window with a low sill. Otis reached out and opened the blinds, because the apartment was on the twenty-eighth floor and he could peer eastward for miles, past the towers of the Triborough Bridge, watching Queens disappear in the haze. Far away was a shining jet, circling for a landing at Kennedy. Jeffrey went slowly and Otis tried to relax. After a couple of minutes he saw the jet again, still circling clockwise, and wondered why it didn't land. The lights on its wingtips flashed on and off. At this moment, he thought, Duane was probably boarding his wife. The idea was disgusting but Otis hoped they got it over with, because then Duane would go away. Duane made him nervous, things were already balanced too perilously. Jeffrey's fingers were twined in his hair, pushing his face down. Otis rolled his eyes to the tops of their sockets and saw the plane crawl past above him. The King of Saudi Arabia was visiting the UN, he remembered. He expected the *Times* to carry rumors of a Mideast settlement, and was counting on that to help Breitbart's oils. If he was lucky the rally would let him pay back Geller. Beyond that, if the oils held until dividends were paid he would dump them and cut his losses. He had a picture of himself in prison, Sandra and Duane coming to visit him, meeting him in a long room and talking to him through a heavy wire screen. Jeffrey shouted. Lights pulsing at its wingtips, high and calm, the jet circled.

Otis drove home in the early dark, his high beams picking up the reflectors on the guard rails. The market had been mugged again. All it would take for him to go to jail was a call from Geller, demanding liquidity. He remembered he had promised to look into a job for Duane. Otis wished he were driving anywhere else. He knew the country held a vast spiderweb of roads, but felt drawn to his own house as though he had no will, to where Sandra and Duane, sipping highballs, were composing themselves to wait for him.

Sandra sat alone. The kitchen was dark now and she had stopped crying. Still she leaned forward on the table, cradling her head in her arms. She had been standing outside Duane's door when it opened suddenly and he stumbled out to the bathroom, while she fled back to her bedroom and locked herself in. Sandra was sure he understood what she had been about to do, and he had seemed silent and cold all day. She hadn't been surprised when, at nightfall, he had told her he had to go. To punish herself, she pictured him walking away through the dark, his hands and lean shoulders relaxing at the thought of having escaped her.

Duane had gotten a ride immediately. He stared out at the dark, unable to make conversation. Each time a car passed going the other way he peered after it, hoping for a last look at Otis's Mercedes. He guessed he would never see Otis or Sandra again, not after what had happened this morning. She had stood listening there outside his door while he lay panting on the bed, relieving his wretchedness into first one enormous cup, then the other, of the brassiere she had found missing from her dresser. Though she had said nothing his shame was unbearable. Duane felt that by visiting Sandra and Otis he had given himself a lifelong wound. Car after car swept by on the other side of the highway, heading for garages in Westchester and Connecticut. He strained his eyes for the Mercedes, but he never saw it, and after a while he decided it was no use breaking his heart.

# Harry and Maury

HARRY SUGARMAN HAD HAD A stroke. During his weeks in the hospital and months at the rehabilitation center—in which time his brother Maury had never come to see him—his only brother—not once—he had barely begun to regain the use of his right hand, arm, and leg. Leaning on a tubular metal walker, he could make it to the end of the hall and back. His speech remained slurred, so that he preferred not to talk, especially since he often couldn't think of the word he wanted.

He was a fighter, a scrapper, people told him, as they stood beside his bed, their heads shaking in wonder. He was sure one hell of a tough cookie. If they were in his place they wouldn't have one-tenth his spirit. Harry despised their encouragement—what did such bigmouths know about suffering? But he often believed that it was true, he was a fighter, or anyway a plugger, and was going to recover no matter what.

Yet he protested when his wife told him, trailing her fingernails back and forth across his sweaty forehead, that

*169*

she was going to take him home. "I think it's too early," he said.

"What?" Bea asked, bending over him in a way that made him dizzy.

"Too early."

"Early?"

"Yes."

"Mrs. Dedomenico will still be there," she said soothingly. Mrs. Dedomenico was the private nurse he liked best, because she was strong enough to lift him easily and because she rarely spoke.

Harry gave up. He knew he was out of touch with the economics of the situation, couldn't remember what his insurance covered and was afraid to ask. But he felt that in leaving the rehabilitation center, which had trained personnel and emergency equipment, he was risking death. Why wouldn't they leave a party where he was, along with all the others who had suffered strokes, leave him where he belonged for now, instead of making him come home?

It wasn't even his own home. As Bea and Mrs. Dedomenico eased his wheelchair from the hired ambulance and slowly up the front walk, he closed his eyes. A door opened and he heard footsteps on the porch. "Harry, terrific," said the voice of Sydelle, his brother Maury's wife. "How are you?" Sydelle and Maury owned the house and lived on the first floor. Harry and Bea lived in the second-floor apartment and paid rent.

"Tired," he answered.

"Tighter?" Sydelle asked.

"Tired."

"A tiger. You sure are, Harry."

"Tired," said Mrs. Dedomenico. "Let's get him up those stairs."

Sugarman and Sugarman were accountants in New Haven. Harry, the elder by eight years, was delicately slim, weak-eyed and slightly deaf in his later years. He carried his aquiline face thrust forward, as though his hearing aid and heavy eyeglasses had overburdened his thin, mottled neck. Nevertheless people had often said that he seemed youthful, even boyish, declaring disbelief that he could really be Maury's senior. That was carrying the compliment further than Harry appreciated. It had led him to answer the telephone in a deeper voice, harsher and more impatient, than was natural for him, though he would then feel embarrassed if the caller was anyone he knew.

It was his brother, who Bea said looked like an overripe tomato, who had seemed the one for a stroke or coronary. Each year Maury's tie had appeared smaller upon his swelling shirt front, and he always drove even the three blocks from their office to the restaurant where Harry walked for lunch. But Maury had had the same luck with his health as with his investments in real estate. Harry's own investments had been in long-term bonds, because he couldn't see himself as a landlord, and inflation had eaten half his principal.

Now he would end his life paying rent to his younger brother. Cheap rent, Maury would sometimes remind him angrily, working the subject around to that when they were arguing about something completely different. He would jab his cigar at the air between them, screwing up his eyes, as though Harry's rent were something tiny and he were trying to knock off his cigar ash against it. *Nominal* rent, Maury would almost squeal, squeezing out the word as though his own generosity amazed him. But it was rent on a place that Harry had never liked, not for an hour, or ever felt was his own home.

From his bed, he could hear Bea and Mrs. Dedomenico having tea in the kitchen. The bedroom, like every other room in the apartment, was a little too small, as though intended for a child. His closet door was ajar, and as Harry watched it he grew angry. "Bea," he called.

He felt pleased when he heard Bea and Mrs. Dedomenico get up immediately. He liked the concerned sound of their chairs scraping backward from the table, their footsteps hurrying down the hall. "Sweetie," his wife said with relief, when she saw him sitting up against his pillows. "Are you comfortable?"

"Shut the door."

Mrs. Dedomenico began to close the door to the hall. "No," Bea said, "the closet door. He always wants it closed. He's so meticulous about his things." She smiled at Harry and opened the closet door wide. "See, sweetie? All okay."

Harry peered. He loved clothes, had loved buying them. Each morning, selecting his outfit had made him feel that the day held hope. In bed at night, he had pictured his clothes awaiting him patiently on their hangers; close to sleep, he had thought of them as his family. Below the garments were tubular metal racks supporting many pairs of shoes—dusty now, he supposed. He had always been vain and at the same time a little ashamed about the smallness of his feet. It had pleased him, though he had never said so to anyone, that even with shoes on he could step into his trousers easily.

"Shut," he said, and waved his left hand.

As Bea closed the closet door he heard someone enter the apartment, and a minute later Sydelle walked in with Mrs. Rappaport, a neighbor. "Harry, I can't tell you how tremendous you look," Sydelle said.

"Amazing," Mrs. Rappaport agreed.

"Doesn't he look—" Sydelle raised her head and held one hand to her cheek as she searched for the word, then dug an elbow at the air beside her and broke into a little dance step to show how peppy Harry looked. It must have been a thousand times, Harry thought, that he had seen her do that little dance. It seemed strange to him that in all the years he had had his strength he had never once asked her to cut it out.

"How is he feeling"—Mrs. Rappaport paused delicately—"otherwise?"

"Only a little confused," Sydelle said.

"It's the strangeness of being home," said Bea.

"I called Maury," Sydelle said, taking Harry's limp right hand. "He had a funeral today, but I left for him to come home as soon as he's back. I called the children too, and of course they're coming to see you. Is that okay?" She turned to Bea. "It's okay if the children come?"

"Of course. Isn't it?" Bea asked Mrs. Dedomenico.

"Is it okay?" Mrs. Dedomenico asked him.

"About time," he said. "Maury."

"Don't give your brother hell," Sydelle begged. She was still holding his weakened hand, and began stroking its fingers. "The way he's suffered for you."

"What can we say?" Bea asked. "Harry was very hurt."

"Maury was *burning* to come. But he couldn't set foot in that hospital, he couldn't bear it. Harry was like a fallen god to him."

"What's past is past," said Bea. "But something like that a person doesn't forget."

"Never," said Harry.

"Don't break his heart more than it's already broken," Sydelle said. "So many of his friends have gone, lately."

"Forgive," Mrs. Rappaport urged.

Harry was beginning to feel queasy. "Bea," he said. He stopped, unable to remember the name for what it was he wanted.

"A tissue?" Bea asked.

"His urinal, maybe," said Sydelle.

"No," said Harry sharply. He raised his left hand and pantomimed drinking from a glass.

"A cup of tea," Mrs. Rappaport pounced.

"One of these," Harry said. And then he said, knowing it was wrong, "Up."

"Water?" said Bea. "And Bufferin?"

"No," Harry told her impatiently. He suddenly felt so furious at her stupidity that he frightened himself—his doctor had said to stay calm if he wanted to live.

"7-Up," explained Mrs. Dedomenico. "Or ginger ale. Sometimes it settles his stomach."

He had finished his ginger ale and was burping painfully when he heard the children arrive: Maury's son Arthur, Arthur's wife Carol, and their daughter Naomi. Arthur was an accountant too, but worked only part time for Sugarman and Sugarman. The rest of the time he played trombone in the orchestras of Broadway musicals, riding back and forth on the train and sometimes staying for days at a friend's apartment in the city.

But now Arthur's life would change, Harry guessed. Though nobody had even hinted at the subject, Harry was afraid that he himself was done working, and that Maury would want Arthur to come in as a full partner. Harry had already decided not to object as he had in the past when this subject came up. All he wanted in return was to stay alive, feel that he had his wits, recover his speech and preferably the grip of his right hand. A strong right leg would be fine too but if that didn't come back he wasn't going to complain. In the deal as he saw it now, Harry was willing to give up the leg and for Arthur to become a partner.

"Uncle Harry's lying down?" asked Arthur's voice. Soon everybody came crowding into Harry's bedroom, and the three who had just arrived kissed him. First tall Arthur, with those big eyes always so wide open that they seemed stupid, bending to grip Harry's shoulders and touch their temples together before giving him a quick kiss on the cheekbone. Then Carol, looking heavier—pregnant again? Harry couldn't remember whether he had been told that or not. He wouldn't risk a comment. Finally Naomi, a chubby doll who made Harry think of the child he and Bea had wanted long ago.

"Pop'll be home any minute," Arthur assured him, sitting on the edge of the bed. The springs shifted, and Harry stiffened so as not to roll toward his nephew. "It's a funeral. He felt he had to ride out to the cemetery."

"Who?"

"Jack Blum." Arthur scratched an ear, then glanced at his fingernail.

Harry shook his head, shocked. Jack Blum was a tax lawyer they had worked with often, a man in the prime of life. "Nobody told me."

"What?"

"Nobody told him," Sydelle said.

"I asked them not to," said Bea. "Not until you were home."

Harry nodded. He understood that they had been

afraid of panicking him, afraid he might refuse to be moved.

There was a silence. Then Carol said cheerfully, "Uncle Harry. We'll be at the shore again this year." She leaned forward, smiling, speaking louder than necessary. Not a beautiful girl, but nice, Harry had always thought. He wondered whether Arthur cheated on her, the way Maury had on Sydelle. "You'll come out, won't you?" Carol asked. "When you're taking little walks it'll be prettier than around here."

"Safer," said Arthur. "This neighborhood here, you'll get mugged like Lou Meyer."

"Lou?"

"While you were in the hospital. Seventeen stitches."

"Now he and Ida don't go for their walks in the evening," Sydelle said. "I think they walked every night since they were married."

Harry felt frightened, but unwilling to show it. Staying at the shore with Arthur was out, as far as he was concerned. "I'll give them this, they get cute," he said. Spreading and stiffening the fingers of his left hand, he jabbed them toward the eyes of an imaginary mugger.

In the silence that followed he saw Naomi look questioningly at her mother, and felt that his gesture had been foolish, flat on his back as he was. "Let's let Harry rest now," Bea said.

"Pop'll be home any minute," Arthur promised. He told Harry, "You look ready for a nap."

"Yes," said Bea. "Try to sleep. We'll wait for Maury in the kitchen. Afterward I have lovely cold chicken."

The last to stand and turn in the doorway was Naomi. "Go to sleep, Uncle Harry," she said, in the intonations of an adult speaking to a child. "Grampa's coming soon."

Maury was in the house, Harry could sense at once when he awoke. How long could he have slept, after lying awake so many minutes listening to the low voices in the kitchen, falling and rising and shushing each other? His room was dim with the light of the end of afternoon. He had soaked his pillowcase with sweat, and now he needed his urinal badly.

His brother's deep voice rumbled in the kitchen, but Harry couldn't understand the words. The idea of seeing Maury after so long moved him powerfully, and he realized with shame that he no longer felt the indignation that was his by right. Nevertheless he couldn't let Maury off so easily. "Bea," he called, but only a croak came out. Squeezing down a sudden little balloon of terror, he cleared his throat and called louder.

There were many footsteps in the hall. Bea came in, with a grinning Maury right behind her, and behind him the others.

"Heschel," said Maury. It was Harry's childhood name, which nobody else called him. Maury held out his right hand and Harry, angry at himself for being unable to resist, met it with his left. But he was still not going to say hello.

Bea was wiping his face with a damp washcloth. "Can I

take your pillow for a second?" she asked him. "I'll give you a fresh case."

"Where's Mrs. Dedomenico?" he demanded.

"She went home. She'll be back in the morning. I'll look after you tonight."

"No," he said, frightened.

"What's wrong, Heschel?" Maury asked. I don't know what's going on here, his tone said, but I'm on your side.

Harry didn't even look at him. "He's used to having a private nurse," said Mrs. Rappaport sympathetically.

"But Dr. Tornillo and Dr. Clark both said he'd be fine without," Bea added quickly.

"My brother wants a private nurse he gets one," said Maury. He glared at everyone in turn. "This is on me. What is there, an agency?"

"You're interfering," said Sydelle.

"Heschel, you want a nurse?"

Harry nodded shortly.

"Fine." Maury put his fists on his hips, sticking out his stomach. "You're getting one."

"Bea," said Harry. "The urinal." His bladder was almost bursting.

"What did he say?" Maury asked.

"He wants his urinal," said Bea. She picked up the steel bottle, but instead of handing it to Harry—whose urge to go became still greater at the sight of it—she paused in embarrassment. "Maybe everyone would step outside for a minute," she said.

Maury took the urinal out of her hands. "I'll give it to

him. You go call the best nurse they have. The best, you tell them." And he herded everyone out of the room, shutting the door behind them.

Then he handed the urinal to Harry, who fumbled it into place just in time. While Harry relieved himself, Maury politely walked to the window and stood looking out at the deepening dusk. "That must feel pretty good," he said. "I can't hold it either, the way I used to."

"I can hold it," Harry said angrily.

"Repeat that?"

"I can hold it."

"Course you can hold it, Hesch. I know you can."

Maury seemed completely natural, but tired. Harry thought he was looking terrible, like a man who'd been talking and working and eating too much and sleeping badly. He fought down a surge of concern, reminding himself who was sick. Yet he kept having the impulse to apologize for adding to his brother's troubles.

"You heard about Jack Blum," said Maury. He turned from the window and faced Harry, shoulders slumped, hands jammed into his pockets as though he had found something there to lean on. "This was a real tragedy. He and Selma had just come back from Boca Raton. They'd put down a payment on a condominium. Jack was so proud, she kept telling me. Heschel, she cried in my arms."

"Heart?" Harry asked.

"What else? A man in perfect health the day before. I'm glad you missed this one."

"A young man."

"Sixty-six. Listen, Heschel. The funeral was all women. Half-a-dozen men tops."

They were both silent. Harry agreed, it was good that he had not been there, lonely among the widows of so many friends who had died. How many men did you know who were widowers? Maybe two or three. He had often wondered why the women lived longer, and he resented it.

"Hesch, you through with the bottle?"

Harry shook his head quickly.

"Fine, keep it. Sometimes I stand there five minutes, these days. I wrap it in toilet paper, afterwards."

"Prostate."

"Of course prostate. I'm not going in until I have to. Danny Fuchs? You heard?"

"No."

"This was also while you were sick. Gallstones, Danny went in for. While he was on the operating table—*while he was on the table, Hesch*—a heart attack. Bingo."

Harry shook his head. Now that Maury reminded him, he seemed to remember hearing the story. And that reminded him of something else he had heard. "Abe Schneider died," he said.

"Attaboy, Heschel," said Maury, smiling unhappily. "You remember. For Abe it was a release, like Joe Rosen last year."

Harry nodded. "Remember Sam Glass?"

"Once more, Heschel."

"Sam Glass."

Maury smiled again. "You're going back a long way now, Hesch."

"Killed himself."

"Fifteen, sixteen years ago. But his widow was there too. Remember Leonore?"

"Sure."

"She was there. And Ruth Siegel and Natalie Rosen, Rosenbloom, Rosen—"

"Bluth."

"Rosenbluth. Remember Dave? Remember Phil?"

"Sure," said Harry. He could see them as well as though they were there in the room next to Maury, who still stood with his hands in his pockets. It had now grown so dark that Harry couldn't see his expression. Neither spoke for a minute, and Harry felt that this was the moment when Maury would say, Heschel—I didn't come to the hospital. I was wrong. You know how much I love you. And in reply Harry would give a little grunt, part condemnation and part dismissal, as though Maury had been wrong but, between brothers, who could hold a grudge. But now Maury remained silent, and after a minute sighed and began to pace. And Bea knocked on the door, calling, "All right in there?"

"Yeah," said Maury. "Heschel, you done?"

Harry handed him the urinal without answering.

"Okay, come in," said Maury.

The door opened and everyone came crowding back

into the room. "Why so dark?" Sydelle demanded. The ceiling fixture seemed to ignite the air, and Harry squinted. "Give me that," Sydelle said, taking the urinal from Maury.

"Listen, we'll all have supper now," Bea said. "Let's leave Harry alone. This is his first day home and it's been too much."

"Of course," said Arthur. "Uncle Harry, we'll say good night."

"Remember, we want you to come to us out at the shore," said Carol.

But he knew he would not be able to sleep unless they gave him the round things, the things in the bottle, the little things that tasted bitter.

"Two," he said.

"What was that?" Sydelle asked.

He couldn't remember the word.

"Maybe he's too cold," suggested Arthur. "Give him a blanket."

Then, with a burst of pride, he did remember. But as he heard himself say it, "Two pillows," he wanted to weep with rage—it was wrong. Bea brought another pillow, and he cried "No!"

She backed away, holding the pillow to her chest. "Let's all just go out now," she said softly. There was an edging toward the door. Harry saw hands begin to rise, to wave goodbye.

But Maury was leaning back, sticking out his stomach,

panting lightly. "Now hold on," he demanded. His voice had a new jocular edge that put Harry on guard. "Where's everyone running to?"

"Harry needs some peace and quiet," Bea said.

"Maury, he's tired," said Sydelle. "All this commotion is confusing."

"Now just hold on," Maury said. He was leaning to his left, and Harry saw his right hand go back and remove his wallet from his hip pocket. "Heschel understands more than you think. He's got all his beans." Maury drew three bills from his wallet and held them out to Harry. A one, a ten, a twenty. "Which would you rather have," he demanded.

Harry hesitated, suspicious. It was a trick, of course. Maury loved to trick you. But Harry saw that if he didn't choose they would think he couldn't. He pointed to the twenty.

"Right," said Maury. "And it's yours." And his thick fingers stuffed the twenty into the breast pocket of Harry's pajamas.

It was only when Arthur laughed outright, and Harry saw that Bea and Sydelle and Carol and Mrs. Rappaport had broken into smiles of applause, that he realized the way his brother had shamed him. He shot Maury a look of hate. But what he saw on Maury's gray face was not the scornful triumph he dreaded. It was relief, relief and pride—what you'd expect if Maury had learned that he himself had all his beans. So again Harry was unsure what to feel. He shut his eyes against the glare of the ceiling light. They were right, he was getting confused. That made him nervous, partly because he guessed it would be okay, it wouldn't matter at all, if he never understood anything again.

# Amarillo

S TEVEN KARPILOW WAS INTENSELY interested in science. Anyway, that was the phrase his mother always used, a phrase Steven disliked without being sure why—"intensely interested." For his eleventh birthday she had given him a bird book and binoculars.

He knelt now at the dining room window, squinting through the binoculars across the long downhill sweep of the back lawn. A blurry fringe flicked down and up—his eyelashes—and the circle bounding his field of vision pulled apart into two overlapping ones, like the picture in his science book of an amoeba dividing. He tried again to focus on Carl's house.

Though Carl was a neighbor, he lived in a different neighborhood. You could tell when you walked down Steven's smooth back lawn, hopped the little stream at the bottom that trickled out of one culvert and disappeared into another, and started up Carl's back lawn, ugly with crabgrass and dog turds. Carl's house was like the others on its street, a little old place with peeling paint and roof of ripped tarpaper. Steven's own street had been carved out of the woods only a few years ago, and some of the spreading houses still didn't have their lawns grown in. The garages were double, with doors that rose in response to a clicker people carried in their cars.

For July, the morning was nice and cool. He and Carl had planned a bike ride to pick up a rat for the long, glossy indigo snake Steven had in his basement. The snake—a female, according to the packing slip—had just come in a box from Amarillo, Texas, and Amarillo was what he had named her. He was surprised by her dry smoothness when you stroked her, the strength of her body as she twisted in your hands.

Was it still too early to go and knock on Carl's door? It was practically nine. But he felt he had to be extra careful with the Pruitts. He was afraid of intruding on them, on some awful problem they might be having.

Besides, Carl himself made Steven feel shy. Carl was a year older, already in junior high, a lean and silent blond. His silence gave him a power that Steven feared. You never knew what he was thinking, and whatever you were thinking, if you mentioned it, didn't interest him at all.

The place they had to go for the rat was a long and hilly distance away. Steven pedaled easily on his ten-speed, but Carl sweated and panted on his heavy old Schwinn, which he used for his paper route—the kind of bike nobody rode anymore—it had fat tires and no gears at all. You could hear rubber rubbing on metal each time the wheels turned, and the chain rattling in the chain guard. Steven found it first embarrassing, then irritating, going slowly enough to stay together.

The trees and bushes were loud with birds—it seemed to Steven that he had never heard and seen so many in his life. But Carl, pumping along doggedly, took no notice of them at all. Coming to the top of the worst hill, he grew red in the face, and for the last stretch had to get off and walk his bike. Steven rode in rolling circles around him, like the overlapping O's his mother made him practice for his penmanship.

Carl was staring straight ahead. Steven finally couldn't stand it. "Hey," he said. "Let's switch a while."

Wordlessly, Carl laid his bike down by the roadside—it had no kickstand—and waited.

Steven dismounted and raised Carl's heavy bike with difficulty. From here on it was mostly downhill. Even so, he was shocked at how hard the thing was to pedal. Descending the next hill he stood up to pump, gaining all the speed he could. Nevertheless, Carl came breezing past him, arms serenely folded. In a moment he was going faster than Steven had ever dared—and no hands. Steven wanted to shout a warning, but stopped himself because it would sound foolish. Then he did yell.

It was too late. Carl didn't seem to hit a bump or pothole, but just as he reached the bottom of the hill he and the bike went pitching over and sliding along the blacktop. "Hey! You okay?" Steven yelled automatically, coasting to a stop, terrified. He was certain Carl was terribly injured, maybe dead, and it was his fault. The police would be called. No college would ever take him now, no matter how hard he worked in high school.

But Carl just stood up and brushed himself off. He was scraped raw on both forearms, the blood oozing through, but he didn't seem to notice. "Shit," he said disgustedly. "It rides crooked. Gimme mine."

"Jeez, are you okay?"

"Shit."

They got back on their own bikes, but Steven's wheels locked in place after half a revolution. Looking down, he saw that the front one was bent way out of shape. He was stuck, miles from home. Now that he knew that Carl was all right, he felt furious at him. "You broke it," he said bitterly. "Whyja go so fast?"

Carl just stared at him. Then he said, "Get off." Steven did. Carl grabbed the wheel with both hands, put his foot against the bent section, pulled until ropes stood out on his red-stippled arms, and slowly the wheel came back into round.

Full of fear and anger and an amazement that was like love, Steven climbed back on. The bike still rode with difficulty, and made a terrible noise with each turn of the wheels, but it rode. Even broken like this, Steven realized, it was easier to pedal than Carl's.

Johnson's Rat Farm raised them for laboratories, every one of them pure white with pink-red eyes. In a barn that seemed immensely long, reeking of ammonia, tier on tier of cages rose to the ceiling. Each cage was so full of rats that they were crawling over each other, and Steven found the continuous squeaking nearly deafening.

"You maybe want a little fella," said Mr. Johnson, reaching into a cage and pulling out a fuzzy thing shorter than his thumb. He held it in mid-air by its tail. It stupidly splayed its four legs and wiggled them about, arching its body and squealing fiercely.

"This is a pretty big snake," Steven said loudly, his hands over his ears.

"Well, okay," said Mr. Johnson, and pulled out a larger rat from the next tier. Steven held open the canvas sack he had brought in his saddlebag, and Mr. Johnson dropped the rat in. "That one's fifty cents," he said.

Carl, hands in pockets, had gone straight to the dim far end of the barn, and now came easing back. "What about one of those big bastards down there," he said. At this language Mr. Johnson looked disapproving, and Steven felt ashamed of his friend, and of himself for bringing Carl along.

Halfway home, the grating got worse. Steven grew afraid that he was damaging his bike more, riding it when it was in this shape. "I've gotta stop," he said. "I'm gonna push it." Carl said nothing but stopped beside him. It always surprised Steven when Carl followed his lead like this—even that Carl, who was so sure of himself, wanted to be with him at all. "His parents send him over," Steven's mother had said cruelly. "They're tickled to death that he has a friend like you."

Though it was now close to midday, birds were still singing along the roadside. "There's a blue jay," Steven said once, and, another time, "Was that a hummingbird?" Carl did not respond. The blood was dry now on his arms, dull and brownish in the sun, patterned in long clouds and continents. Inside Steven's saddlebag, the rat squealed and scrabbled about in its sack.

They walked along in silence, and the wonder of how many birds there were grew on Steven—birds in the bushes, in the trees, thick in the woods that stretched back on both sides of the road, birds hopping on lawns when they came to houses, birds flying overhead. There were uncountable birds at all points of the compass, he realized, swarms of bright birds filling the jungles, great clouds of seabirds along the shores. Pushing his bike, he almost ran over a decaying one on the roadside. He held his breath as he passed, feeling strange.

Though why should he? With so many birds, weren't there naturally going to be a lot of dead ones? But that was just the thing—there *weren't* a lot. You saw them dead only once in a while. And there were so many of them alive, it seemed—it seemed now to Steven—that the whole world should be piled high with the bodies of those that had died.

They were coming into Carl's neighborhood, turning onto the long street lined with little houses that had once been identical. Varying styles of dilapidation now gave each of them a personality. Some had boarded windows, some had wildly overgrown lawns. One had broken-down cars filling its driveway and most of its front yard. Children's bicycles and tricycles and riding toys cluttered the little front porches, the lawns, the rutted edges of the asphalt street—there were no sidewalks or curbs.

What could account for it? You should have seen dead birds everywhere, heaps and banks of them—did they fling themselves into the ocean, into rivers and lakes, when they knew they were dying? That was unscientific. Maybe cats and dogs ate them, but Steven doubted it, you saw cats and dogs all the time, and they were rarely eating birds. Could every property-owner be removing whatever birds died on his property? You almost never saw that happening, either. Then where were they?

"You gonna feed it now?" Carl asked.

"Sure," Steven said. They were coming to Carl's house, at the end of the row. A tiny, dirty child wearing only underpants was playing out in front with a shovel and pail. Steven had never learned the names of Carl's youngest brothers and sisters, and wasn't even sure whether this one was a boy or a girl. Carl's mother was sitting on the front step, watching the child. The thing that still shocked Steven, though this was nothing new, was seeing Carl's father there too—a man at home in the middle of the day, a weekday, and just sitting. Mr. Pruitt was out of work, Steven's father had explained, which had made Steven's mother frown and shake her head, signaling that she would have liked to explain further, but was keeping herself silent. Carl laid down his bike. "We're gonna feed a rat to the snake," he said. His mother yelled, "Don't you get bit!"

In Steven's dark, cool basement, the brightest thing was the iridescent Amarillo, shining expensively under her heat lamp. "Let's hold 'em nose to nose," Carl said.

"You don't handle them just before feeding," Steven told him. He slid back the glass top and emptied the rat from its sack. It quickly dashed the length of the tank, right in front of Amarillo, who hissed and drew back, puffing up her body.

"He's *scared,*" Carl crowed.

"She just has to get used to it," said Steven, but felt himself blushing with shame.

They stepped back and sat on the cement floor, holding still, watching. The rat explored every inch of the cage. Amarillo showed no interest, except to draw back sharply when the rat crawled over her gleaming body.

"Lemme do it," Carl said. He reached in and grabbed the rat, which turned and bit him. "Bastard," he said, letting go. He grabbed again and this time caught the rat by the tail. He swung it enticingly before the snake, which followed its motions carefully but would not strike at it. "Come on, you fuck," said Carl. "Think he'd eat a bird?"

"We better take out the rat." It made Steven nervous, how aggressive and unafraid the rat seemed, and how timid Amarillo was.

"Leave it in while we get a bird," Carl said. "Let him get used to it."

Steven thought Carl would know some smart ways of catching a bird, but Carl only shrugged and watched as

Steven propped up a bucket with a clothespin, spread bread crumbs on the grass beneath, then ran a string from the clothespin back to the house and in through the dining room window. It was then that Carl took over, insisting on holding the string. And it was Carl who yanked the string at exactly the right time, after they'd been waiting only a few minutes, and led the way out of the house with a wild shout, to where a starling was banging itself around inside the bucket.

When they got back to the cellar the rat was drinking the snake's water, the snake coiled as far away as possible. But the moment Carl dropped in the fluttering bird, Amarillo lunged. She threw herself forward savagely, striking and missing, striking and missing again, smashing her nose against the glass, while the bird squawked and tried to fly, beating its wings at the sides and top of the tank, and Carl shouted, "All *right!* All *right!*", and Steven watched in horror—he'd expected it to be over in a moment—until the snake seized the bird at last.

"He'll never get that thing down," said Carl. Amarillo's head looked tiny, clamped onto the bird's body, and the starling was still struggling fiercely, its feathers fluffed so it looked gigantic, squawking in a way that made Steven cover his ears. Amarillo flung shining loops over her prey and began working her jaws around to the bird's head. The bird's struggles grew weaker but not its cries. Even as its head began disappearing into the snake's mouth, Steven could still hear it. After half an hour there was only a great, sick-looking bulge. Amarillo lay torpid. "All ri-i-ight," Carl sighed.

That night, Steven was kept awake by the birds in the trees outside his window. It was years since he had been afraid of the dark—there was nothing to be afraid of, the world didn't change at night. But something, he didn't know what, was bothering him. Again, he wondered why the earth wasn't blanketed with dead birds—and dead everything else, come to think of it. How could all the things that died get tucked out of sight so well? Where was there room to put them all? But even that wasn't what was bothering him, it was something else.

And when he woke up in the gray pre-dawn, the trees pattering beneath a soft rain, he knew with his first thought exactly what it was. They had left the rat in with the snake. You weren't supposed to do that. A rat could kill a snake that wasn't hungry, a snake that was sleeping off a meal.

He hurried down to the basement, and there it was, in the bright light of the heat lamp—Amarillo, still bloated from the bird, her head half eaten away. In a corner of the tank crouched the rat, grooming itself.

It was Carl's fault! It was Carl who had said to leave the rat in, and Steven, like a fool—he felt like hitting his head on the floor—had done it. He dashed up the cellar stairs, through the kitchen and out the back door and down the lawn, to knock, knock and yell, until Carl came, and show him the awful thing that had happened.

But as he approached the little stream that separated the

back yards, he slowed and stopped. A figure was moving across the lawn behind the Pruitts' house. First he thought it was Carl, up early for his paper route, and was ready to call him. But then he saw that it was Mr. Pruitt, and that the bag over his shoulder held something heavier than newspapers. Mr. Pruitt looked exhausted. He climbed his back steps with difficulty and went inside.

Steven stepped across the stream and silently up the sodden lawn. The rain beating on the Pruitts' house grew louder as he approached. On tiptoe, he was just able to look in at the kitchen window, where a light shone.

There was Mr. Pruitt, sunk in a chair as though the last of his strength were gone forever, water draining from him and collecting in pools on the floor. Mrs. Pruitt was emptying the bag he had brought onto the table. They were mostly sparrows and starlings, muddy from where they had lain, and one enormous crow, and some that Steven couldn't remember ever seeing before. There were several dead squirrels spilled among them, and a crushed turtle.

Steven raised his eyes and looked down the row of shabby little houses. In many of the poor people's kitchens, he saw now, lights were burning. The idea that came to him then was totally unscientific, and in later years he would wonder how it had entered his head. But he would never regret—when he was an old man he would remember it as the best thing he'd done in his life—going home at once, and taking his still Amarillo into the woods, and burying her so deep that time and change would never touch her.

In 1980 the Howard Heinz Endowment of Pittsburgh, Pennsylvania, through a grant to the University of Pittsburgh Press, created the Drue Heinz Literature Prize to recognize and encourage the writing of short fiction.

*The Death of Descartes,* by David Bosworth, 1981
*Dancing for Men,* by Robley Wilson, Jr., 1982
*Private Parties,* by Jonathan Penner, 1983